THE FISH OF A THOUSAND CASTS

The Fish of a Thousand Casts

Tales of Mischief and Mayhem in the Great Outdoors

Steven Hutchins

Copyright © 2002 by Steven Hutchins.

Cover Art: Julie Anderson

Back Cover Photo: Stephenie Phelps-Hutchins

Library of Congress Number: 2002091558
ISBN: Hardcover   1-4010-5492-7
        Softcover   1-4010-5491-9

All rights reserved. No part of this book may be reproduced or transmitted in any form or by any means, electronic or mechanical, including photocopying, recording, or by any information storage and retrieval system, without permission in writing from the copyright owner.

This is a work of fiction. Names, characters, places and incidents either are the product of the author's imagination or are used fictitiously, and any resemblance to any actual persons, living or dead, events, or locales is entirely coincidental.

This book was printed in the United States of America.

To order additional copies of this book, contact:
Xlibris Corporation
1-888-795-4274
www.Xlibris.com
Orders@Xlibris.com

Contents

Acknowledgements 9
Forward: Life in the Great Outdoors 11
The Fish of a Thousand Casts 18
Hunting with The Buckmaster 25
Taking The Plunge 33
The Not-So-Perfect Storm 38
The Pine River Plunge 47
Over The River and Through The Woods 56
Moonlight Madness 63
Chuck and . . . DUCK! 70
Courtin' in the K-Zoo Valley 82
The Canoe Race 96
Snow, Steelies and The Big "V" 105
White Tailed Annie's New Tattoo 113
Big Red 125
My Days at Camp Happi-Sissie 133
The Ghost of Tripping Beaver 146
A Little Fresh Air 163
Beef and the Big Buck 172
One of Those Days 181
Death of a Sportsman 189

DEDICATION

This book is humbly dedicated to the memory of my grandfather, LaVern Kramer and my grandmother, Letha Hutchins . . . I miss you both and think of you often.

Acknowledgements

Where Do I begin? I've truly been blessed in my 33 years of life and to thank everyone, would take an entire book in itself!

Stephenie, you are the light of my life. Your patience and understanding as well as your long hours in helping me prepare this manuscript mean more to me than any words can describe. I love you always. You are my one true soul mate. (Note: Dear readers, please don't confuse Steph with "the wife" character that pops up occasionally. *That* parasite, long since extracted, could never hold a candle to my beloved Stephenie!)

Mom and Dad, thank you for the love and support and always believing in me!

Grandma Kramer, you and Grandpa always believed in me... I hope this book does you proud. You mean so much to me...

My family, Norma, Jeff, John, Jerry, Cookie, Andy, Jeremy, Kyle...

Roger Foust and Doug Waldron . . . good friends like you are hard to come by!

Julie Anderson for the cover art, it's exactly what I envisioned!

Tom Campbell, thank you for publishing my work, and allowing me to entertain your readers.

Mike Gnatkowski, Steph and I thank you for the helpful advice and pointers!

Dave Mull, Linda at Midwest Outdoors, Nick Amato . . . thank you!

Patrick F. McManus . . . you are the master, I'm merely a student. Thank you for your years of amazing work . . . it inspired me to create.

Roger and Beth at the Rockford Squire . . . thank you for giving me some valuable experience.

Hans Anderson, Lisa, BK, Diane, Ken and everyone at Kalfact Plastics . . . thank you for putting up with me!

God . . . you have truly blessed me. I live life in your name and glory.

Endorsements: Woods N Water News, Midwest Outdoors, Great Lakes Angler, STS, The Steelhead Site, The Michigan Sportsman, Baldwin Bait & Tackle in Baldwin, Pappy's in Wellston, The Great Lakes Fly Fishing Company in Rockford, Steve's Bait and Tackle in Nunica, Dick Swan and Swan's Custom Rods . . . excellent services provided by reputable and upstanding sportsmen and women!

Forward: Life in the Great Outdoors

My good friend's son recently took an interest in my fishing activities.

"Mom says you fish too much!"

The boy is only seven so I tried to respond in a manner that he would understand. "Tell your mom that she shops too much."

"I wanna fish too much too," he said.

My friend would've been proud if he'd heard that. Unfortunately, he was busy negotiating with his significant other about acquiring some free time to join me on the water.

"But... but... but, honey," he pleaded. "He's not that bad of a person!"

"Not that bad?" his wife screamed. "We just paid off the medical bill from the last time you went with him! Do I need to remind you about that little incident with the sheriff? NO... you're not going!"

I've never understood why so many people are against

the idea of outdoors recreation. So it's not always picture perfect, big deal! Fishing, and hunting for that matter, are perfect ways to keep a youngster, or adult, occupied. What's more productive, vegetating in front of a video game or learning the proper way to fall down a muddy slope without damaging your fishing rod or gun? With the right teaching, the next generation of humanity can learn valuable lessons that not only apply in the outdoors but also in everyday life. When I was old enough to fall down, my Grandma Hutchins put a fishing pole in my hand and taught me the ways of the water. I haven't put the rod down yet! Along the way I've had several people teach me things about the outdoors and everyday something catches my eye that I can put away in the memory bank. How can anyone say, "You fish too much!" or "You hunt too much"? Did anyone ever tell Tiger Woods that he golfs too much? What about Jerry Rice? I suppose he played football too much! For that matter, did anyone ever tell Bill Clinton he chases... well, I suppose his wife did, bad example but you get my point: you can never spend too much time doing productive things!

    I'm a firm believer that outdoor education should be taught in schools. I never had much use for algebra, chemistry, or geometry. I didn't have Attention Deficit Disorder; I had Don't Wanna Know Syndrome. If a teacher started droning on about electrons and molecules I was gone. If they started talking about shooting lines and drift techniques I was all ears. As you can guess, there weren't many lectures about fishing and hunting so you can figure out that my GPA was pretty... uh... non-existent. I did have one teacher who was an avid hunter and he always started class with some sort of hunting tale. That five minute stretch was probably the only time I was mentally present in any class room environment!

    While the rest of my classmates were toiling in the works of Dickens, Shakespeare and Melville, I was deep into the

THE FISH OF A THOUSAND CASTS

works of Mike Gnatkowski, Kenny Darwin, Jim Bedford and Pat McManus (based on my outdoor experiences, his books seemed like "how to's"). Woods N Water News was *my* English book. In math, I understood the concept of 2+2 = 4 but algebra escaped me completely. How many times in the woods do you ask: "If tree X is hanging over river Y then at what point does said fish = Z?" The only math that matters in the woods is 3 points on each horn = 6 points. Enough said. I never did homework. I hated homework. I used to think that homework was the concoction of the anti's or PETA. A sinister plot to keep budding sportsmen out of the woods and off the water. It worked on most, *but not me!*

My life in high school revolved around four things: Fishing, listening to heavy metal music at ungodly decibels, chasing girls and fishing. At that age, I realized that I enjoyed entertaining people, or better yet, being the center of attention. I was a straight "D" student and the "D" stood for "disruptive" and "defiant". I tried to be the class clown... of every class I took! I was sent to the principle's office so many times that I had my own desk there. Heck, my parents got called to the school so much that they had their own personal parking space in the faculty lot! The common thought was that I would amount to... well... nothing. "He just doesn't pay attention," they said. Yes I did! I may not have been able to tell a pronoun from an adjective, but I could sure as hell catch fish in the most adverse conditions. Obviously I paid attention to something. Many of my classmates went on to become Lawyers, Accountants, Engineers, and Business Gurus but how much time do they spend in the outdoors? With their busy schedules it's probably limited. I, on the other hand, have a good job that offers a great deal of free time, write outdoor articles, listen to heavy metal music at ungodly decibels, and CATCH LOTS AND LOTS OF FISH. Who came out ahead in life after all?

My love of the outdoors led me into outdoor writing. I

love being in the outdoors and I love talking about the outdoors; it was a logical move. Ok, maybe not that logical . . . I mean, it wasn't expected. Honestly, it was shocking. Based on my high school GPA it would be safe to conclude that no teacher, or my parents for that matter, would ever expect me to write anything more than "KISS Rules!" on my note book, let alone an article or this book. It was so shocking that one of my former English teachers had to be rushed to the emergency room after he was thumbing through an issue of Woods N Water News and saw one of my articles! Apparently he was in full cardiac arrest and kept gasping, "It can't be! It can't be!" He's doing fine now, but he no longer looks at outdoor magazines . . .

For the record, outdoor writing is not rocket science. Hell, I've proven that! It certainly isn't a wise career choice and I haven't given up my day job. If I did, I'd be in the poorhouse. What it does do, however, is offer a good excuse to spend more time in the outdoors. I used to go round and round with people about the amount of time I spend fishing, camping, etc. Now, I can simply state that I'm a writer and that all the time I spend is "research". I love salmon and steelhead fishing so . . . I do a LOT of "research" on those kinds of articles!

Outdoor writing has many downsides. First, there's what an acquaintance of mine calls, "The Hemingway Effect". How many articles have you read where the author goes into vivid details to paint the picture perfect scene of life in the outdoors? You know, the ones that read like this: "I eased into the gin clear waters. It was cool, yet clung to my legs like silk. As the sun rose brilliantly in the east, I gently launched my fly onto the misty surface of this liquid utopia. The # 12 hand-made Royal Coachman settled like a feather a top the pool. From out of nowhere, a majestic trout engulfed my offering and the battle was on! I attempted to vanquish the mighty leviathan, a lasting bond between man and beast..." Do I need to go on? I can't really find fault with that style of writing because I've been guilty of using it in the past. In fact, the first article I had published started out, "The mist from the St. Joe rose into the air like a poltergeist..." But how *real* is that portrait we try to paint? Honestly... it's a bunch of bull! When the outdoor writer is painting his picture, he leaves out what really happened in his vanquishing of the leviathan. He leaves out the part about locking his keys in his vehicle, falling down a muddy hill, breaking his fly rod, tripping over a log and getting chased for half a mile by a rabid raccoon that lived in the log! The leviathan he vanquished? It didn't bite a # 12 hand-made Royal Coachman... it bit a big ol' leaf worm suspended under a red and white bobber because he left his fly box in the truck! "The Hemingway Effect" is an easy trap to fall into, but hardly realistic! I still do articles like that... can't help it, but I'd much prefer to tackle the realistic side of life in the great outdoors.

Another downside to this is the anonymity that comes with it. You don't have groupies or fan clubs and no one runs up to you and asks for an autograph! The more I think about it, why in hell am I doing this in the first place? It certainly doesn't make me the class clown or the center of attention, as I've always desired... in fact, it stinks! I used to have these fantasies about being recognized. Boy, was I naive. In my mind's eye, I pictured myself on a crowded river. No one is catching a thing... except me. Just as I've vanquished another leviathan (after easing into the gin clear waters blah, blah, blah), a fellow angler comes up to me and says, "Say... aren't you Steve Hutchins, the guy who writes for those magazines? I love your work!" I smile, say "thank you", and begin a wonderful conversation about the great outdoors. Ha! I've since given up on that ever happening! I just continue to write my little stories about falling in the water and breaking bones, content with the obscurity that comes with it. I even have one of those head shot photos that appears beside my name and no one notices!

I take that back. I *was* recognized once. One of my friends, Mean Gene, I'll call him, invited me to float the Muskegon River for steelhead last spring. It was a cold misty day and the fish weren't hitting a thing. We were fishing a deep pool and Mean Gene decided to reposition the boat by raising the anchor and letting us drift for a bit. I wasn't paying attention when he dropped the anchor back down and the sudden stop caught me off balance. I tumbled into the water. The current started to push me down river and as I flailed past the boat, Mean Gene started to reach for the anchor rope so he could retrieve me. At the same time, a huge steelie bit down on his spawn bag. "Look at the size of that thing!" he shouted. Putting the anchor rope back down, he played the monster fish as I drifted down river.

I finally got my footing at a shallow spot around the next bend. The current was swift, took my feet out from under me and I was back to drifting down river. When I fell the second time, my coat inflated with an air pocket and acted like a life preserver. I bobbed merrily down stream, hoping that Mean Gene would hurry up and come get me. It must have been a really long battle because I never saw him. I just kept bobbing along...

Finally, I happened upon a lone angler, in a boat, who was drifting some lures through a pool. As I bobbed up to his boat, he looked into the water and said, "Hello".

"How's it going?" I asked. "Catching anything?"

"Nope... it's been slow," he answered. He rowed his boat a little faster so he could keep up with me and continue our conversation.

"Have you tried a longer leader?" I asked. "Maybe less weight will work."

"Tried all that. Haven't hooked a thing," he said. At that moment he gave me a curious look.

"Say . . . aren't you that guy who writes those stories about falling in the water and breaking bones and stuff?" he asked.

"McManus?" I wondered. I didn't expect anyone to know who *I* was.

"No, not McManus, *he's* funny," the angler clarified. "I'm talking about one of the other guys . . . one who *isn't*."

"Yep, that's me!" I answered, continuing to bob downstream and beaming with pride over finally being recognized.

"By the way, what are you doing just bobbing along like that?" he finally questioned.

"Research!" I quickly said. "Just doing a little research."

Then it hit me. "I eased into the gin clear waters. It was cool, yet clung to my legs like silk." *BULL!* This water's freezing and I fell in! Vanquished leviathan my foot. This is what really happens when you venture into the great outdoors . . .

The Fish of a Thousand Casts

"I have seen the face of evil and . . . it's silver" –*unknown*

The sport of fishing has always been made up of two distinct factions: those who do it for peace and serenity and those who *claim* to do it for peace and serenity. I, unfortunately fall into the latter category. The people who make up the former have never in their sheltered lives been exposed to Steelhead fishing. All thoughts of peace and serenity are quickly smashed into little pieces and tossed unceremoniously out the window once an angler has been given the opportunity to "match wits" with a Steelhead. If you were to ask a casual angler how his day was he might reply, "Oh I didn't catch anything, but golly it was just a nice day to be outdoors." Ask a Steelie chaser and all you'll get is a blank stare and perhaps a muttered expletive or two.

Since the age of 15, I have passionately pursued the Steelhead and can testify that there is no other form of

THE FISH OF A THOUSAND CASTS

enjoyable torture to which it can compare. I'm not trying to dissuade anyone from taking up the sport but to say it is addicting is like saying that heroin is "just another drug". Frustration is the norm, heartbreak a daily occurrence, and each cast becomes a mission in futility that keeps you coming back for more.

To give you the proper perspective on Steelhead fishing, we must venture back to its origins:

Several hundred years ago, Vlad the Impaler and Attila the Hun happened to be discussing the fine art of torture over a few pints of ale. Each came to the realization that, while the torture business had been recently booming, it was starting to show signs of a recession.

"What we need to do, my unwashed companion, is shake up the industry . . . give it new and inventive ways with which to torment," said Mr. Vlad.

"Mmmm, torment good," grunted Attila, in obvious agreement.

"Those fishing people seem to be enjoying themselves a little too much, perhaps we haven't targeted that demographic as aggressively as we should," added the Vlad.

The two plotted and schemed until it was decided that they would charter a fishing trip with some of their "rivals" in the industry. The trip was scheduled for mid February.

Once on the water, Mr. Vlad began practicing his newly patented "hook through the flesh" technique. Attila, on the other hand, had recently acquired a long, slender piece of 98% graphite and was testing its sensitivity on the craniums of his counterparts. One such fellow by the name of "Wiggler" was so intent in his fishing activities that he failed to notice the carnage that was going on around him. He'd hooked a fish that was very large and his determination to bring it aboard the boat had overwhelmed him. Attila made several attempts to get his attention but Wiggler didn't seem to notice the numerous whacks to the back of his head. "I think I've got a big one!" he kept shouting over and over. Attila was so outraged that he finally picked up Wiggler and tossed him overboard.

"Me hit and hit but him not notice," Attila sighed. "He must have *steel head*"

For years and years thereafter, anglers migrated to the water to pay tribute to "Mr. Steel Head" and the sport began to evolve into what it is today. Once, when someone actually caught a fish, it was named after the man for whom they paid tribute. Needless to say, Attila and The Impaler were quite pleased that their efforts had caused grown men to willingly stick hooks in their fingers, whack themselves in the head with long rods and plunge into icy cold water, while pointlessly pursuing an unnamed fish. Even today, Steelhead purists still engage in the centuries old practice of "Stick, Whack, and Plunge".

Despite this newfound insight of the sport, don't believe for a moment that the fish themselves are not a willing participant in this torture.

The Steelhead is commonly referred to as "The Fish of a Thousand Casts". Aptly named, these wily creatures can be present in good numbers but will not hit anything until they're good and ready. They can be in the river so thick that you could walk across them and you'll still end up going home without hooking a thing. Had William Shakespeare been a steelie chaser, I'm sure the famous line would've been "Where for art thou . . . *steelie?*" These fish know what they're doing. They are evil, selfish, and uncaring. Just as an angler is about to give up and go home, a steelie will jump out of the water and say, "Here I am!" The angler will continue his casting ritual until his arm falls off.

One thing Steelhead are famous for is their ability to tease fishermen. An angler will hit the river at 5:00 in the morning and immediately begin hooking Steelhead. He won't land any, but he's drawn into a false illusion that the fish are really hungry and will hit anything. This is all part of the sinister plot. Once the angler is lulled into that illusion, the Steelhead will stop biting. The angler, convinced that they will start biting again, will stand in the same spot and fish non-stop until the sun goes down. He'll leave the river a broken and desolate man but is back at it the next day... casting and casting without a nibble.

Anglers everywhere have spent a millennium trying to figure out the Steelhead. They've inspired downtrodden anglers to form support groups. An Internet site, The Steelhead Site, is a gathering place for hordes of lunatics who share the common bond of steelie insanity. They scream, they yell, and occasionally try to question the circumstances that brought them to this frail condition. After a recent "outing" which was sponsored by the site, my girlfriend Steph commented that our passion for this illogical quest reminded her of a cult! Perhaps, but this is one cult that the FBI wouldn't touch with a ten foot pole!

"Say, you think we ought to investigate that Steelhead cult?" one agent would ask his partner.

"Are you kidding? Those people are nuts!" his partner would reply. "Who knows what they're capable of!"

After years of trying to figure out a Steelhead's rhyme and reason, I've become an expert in knowing that: *there is no rhyme or reason to their behavior!* When you hear an "expert" droning on about water temps, river currents, holding areas, tailouts, thermoclines, weather conditions, moon phases, etc... what we're really trying to say is: "Who knows? I gave up trying to figure out those damn fish a long time ago!"

Steelhead fishing is a daily test of ones faith. I've yet to meet a human being that could withstand the sorrow and heartbreak without looking up to the heavens and screaming "WHY ME?" If the good Lord had sent Job on a Steelhead expedition, He'd have been extremely disappointed with Job's behavior. A perfect example of this is my good friend Wally.

Wally is a solid family man who is highly respected in

both his church and community. He is a man of strong faith, focused, levelheaded, and doesn't drink or smoke. Wally doesn't let much affect him. His cursing vocabulary consists of "Jeez", "Phooey", and "Heavens sake!"—and those are the harsh ones! In other words, he's the kind of human being that steelies love to prey upon.

An excellent outdoorsman, Wally wanted to try his hand at Steelhead fishing. Misery loves company so I gladly volunteered to take him out. Our day on the river began typically. I taught him the ritual of "Stick, Whack, and Plunge" and he seemed to be enjoying himself. The Steelhead sensed this and had a grand scheme planned for him. They'd bite just enough to keep him interested and fight long enough for him to get excited only to break the line and jump out of the water waving "bye-bye". Each broken line was met with a "Jeez, can you believe that?" or "Phooey! Maybe I need some stronger line." As the day wore on, I could see him starting to crack. The steelies toyed with him endlessly. By evening, Wally had taken up smoking, acquired a taste for stiff drink, and was cussing with such fluency that hardened sailors would gasp in awe and give him a standing ovation.

Wally was hooked on the sport and thanked me profusely on the way home. His wife, a good person herself, never liked me after that day and now refers to me as "The Demon". Whenever I call their house and she answers the phone, the conversation goes something like this:

"Hello?" she'll answer cheerfully.

"Hey! Is Wally around?" I'll ask.

"Oh . . . It's . . . *you*. What do you want him for?" she'll hiss. Her voice trembling in an angry tone. "Did you run out of souls to steal?"

"Heh heh heh! Nope, I just wanted to see if he'd like to get out on the river for a little peace and serenity!"

"Peace and Sere—*Is that what you call it?!*" she'll sob.

THE FISH OF A THOUSAND CASTS

"Leave my husband alone!!! He's a good man!"
CLICK!
The Steelhead's power is so intense that it's turned her into an irrational woman. I'm not to blame for the change in her husband, the fish are, but who'd believe that? I've since learned to call him at work and *covertly* plan any upcoming excursions. Wally is a regular participant in a number of adventures, but his attendance is discouraged by his better half. She flat out doesn't like me and views me as a bad influence on her husband. Maybe she's right...

Ultimately, the fishing gods are the ones pulling the strings in this evil plot called steelheading. If, by chance, you have a good day on the river, you can be assured that a stiff price will be paid later. Most of the time the price involves a broken rod, broken leg, or broken spirit.

Last spring, I ventured onto the St. Joe River before dawn. I had the river all to myself and the steelies were biting everything I threw into the water. I'd landed and released twenty or so without incident and developed a false sense that I'd finally outwitted the fishing gods. The weather was beautiful, the fish were plentiful and I hadn't even broken a single line. Evening came and I carefully left the river. I was extremely nervous because I knew that the gods were going to exact a heavy toll on me. As I drove home, *nothing happened*, no car pulling out, no deer running out, nothing. I stopped at a fast food drive—thru to get some dinner, *and the order was correct*. Uh oh, I was getting frantic. What was going to happen? I made it home safely and was extremely relieved to settle into my recliner and watch TV. I'd won! I got away from the fishing gods without paying a price. *HA!*

I bit into my sandwich and felt something crunch. Since when is a Big Mac crunchy? It didn't take long to realize that the cap on my front tooth had broken into several pieces. The fishing gods had their revenge and I now looked like a cross between Alfred E. Neuman and Alfalfa. Steph might've been sympathetic had I not been attempting to curse with a severe lisp.

The next day on the river, a gentleman I knew came up and said hello.

"How'd ya do yesterday?" he asked.

I flashed him a toothless grin and didn't say a word.

"Looks like ya had a good day!" he said.

I noticed the butterfly bandages covering his forehead. "Looks like you did too" I said. "Good luck!"

As he limped away, I went back to my "Stick, Whack, and Plunge" routine. Steelheads never release their prey. In fact, *they've never even heard of catch and release!* Once hooked, you're doomed for life . . .

Hunting with The Buckmaster

Every year thousands of hunters take to the woods to satisfy that ancient yearning to conquer and capture their family's food supply. For some it's a religious experience to which nothing can compare. But when the call of the wild beckons me into the woods, I pretty much ignore it. I'm not a hunter. Hunting and I were not meant to be together. I made every attempt to take up the sport but it just wasn't in the cards.

I'm not opposed to hunting; never have been never will be. It's simply a matter of not having enough time. In addition, my past experience attempting the sport didn't excite me the way that it does others. It doesn't bother me much because I'm a die-hard fisherman. Salmon and Steelhead keep me on the water year round. If I were to go out hunting, that would take away from my precious fishing time.

At one time, I was intrigued with the thought of hunting . . .

Not so long ago, when the leaves began to turn, a strange urge came over me to go deer hunting. The season was a month away so I knew I had to act fast if I was going to submit to nature's call. My next door neighbor, The Buckmaster, had been needling me to go hunting with him. He was a fairly large man with a long black beard who was well known for his hunting knowledge. Because of that knowledge and the way he described his hunting experiences, I fully expected to have a buck come right up, sit down beside me, and give me pointers on the proper way to cook him. With the Buckmaster as my guide, I knew that I would have my deer opening morning and still have time for coffee at the local diner.

The Buckmaster lived for deer hunting; never mind that his only exposure to the outdoors came during the 15-day gun season. He talked hunting 365 days a year and showed off his hunting prowess by displaying numerous, handmade, mounted racks on his living room wall. Yep, right down to his patented "Tan Your Own Hide Kit" and his T-shirt that read "The Buck Stops Here", the man lived for deer hunting.

I agreed to apprentice under his expert tutelage and began the process of turning into a deer hunter.

"We need to get you a hunting license," The Buckmaster stated. "Got your hunter's safety card?"

Uh oh, I did not have my hunter safety card. *I never even took hunter safety.* I grew up in Hillsdale County where hunter safety was a requirement for High School graduation. Somehow, I'd managed to slip through the cracks and was allowed to graduate without it (an obvious oversight). This was a heinous crime; life in Hillsdale County revolved around three things: The County Fair, The Purple Loosestrife Festival and deer hunting. If I told The Buckmaster that I didn't have a hunter safety card I was surely going to be ridiculed and labeled the

THE FISH OF A THOUSAND CASTS

new town fool. Being labeled as the town fool in Hillsdale is the mother of all disgraces so I had to think fast or the Buckmaster was going to get suspicious.

"I lost it," I replied.

"Well, I guess you'll have to take it again," The Buckmaster pointed out. "They're having a course this weekend down at the Gun and Muffin Club"

As that statement was made, The Buckmaster called one of his buddies at the club and secured me a spot in the weekend class.

Saturday morning The Buckmaster drove me out to the Hillsdale County Gun and Muffin Club for "school". The members of this establishment were outdoorsmen, who sponsored a number of outdoor-related activities like hunter safety, bake sales and strippers. The latter being reserved for special events like "keg night", or Friday, as the rest of us call it. The G & M compound was located in a nice country setting complete with a gun range, nature trail, and panfish pond. I entered the classroom and immediately felt out of place. All of my classmates were under the age of 13 and were decked from head to toe in orange "bomber" hats, flannel shirts, and carhart pants. Parents and students alike gawked in disbelief as I entered the room. You'd have thought they'd never seen a 23-year-old with ripped jeans and an Iron Maiden T-shirt in hunter safety before. They take their deer hunting very seriously in Hillsdale County and to them I looked like a slacker. All eyes followed me to my seat in the back of the room and I heard the strange, yet distinct, music that is the theme to "The Twilight Zone"

Both days in the class were pretty uneventful, although there was that little "incident" on the shooting range.

Part of the hunter safety course involves shooting practice out on the gun range; the point being to enforce responsible firearm handling. I figured I was going to clean up in this little test since my young classmates were having a hard time hitting the clay pigeons zipping through the air. My turn finally came up. I stepped into the shooting area with a visible confidence. I raised my shotgun to my shoulder and eased the safety off.

"Pull!" I shouted. I scanned the sky for a clay target, seeing nothing.

"Pull!" I shouted again. Still nothing.

"The launchers jammed," The Buckmaster said. "We'll have to launch em' by hand."

One of the "teachers", a character by the name of Grubby Gary, grabbed some odd looking paddle, placed a target in it and positioned himself about ten feet behind me.

"This will get em' out there!" Grubby Gary said. "Just say the word."

I focused my attention on the sky, raised the gun and shouted the word. Grubby Gary reared back and let the pigeon fly. Apparently he misjudged the trajectory; the impact with my head and the blast of the shotgun were instantaneous. As pieces of the clay missile settled around my feet and smoke drifted from the gun barrel, I began to wander around cross-eyed and dazed. This caused quite a bit of concern as I was still holding the shotgun. Everyone ran for cover and the subsequent panic led one individual to scream, "Take him out, pa! Take him out!"

That little "incident" received quite a bit of attention at the local diner, The Queasy Kitchen, and was talked about for several days afterwards. In spite of all that, I earned my little orange hunter safety card and was able to purchase my hunting license.

Next up on the Buckmaster's agenda was the selection of hunting spots and the building of blinds. Hunting in Hillsdale County takes place in two locations; a cornfield, or somewhere near a cornfield. I was assigned the latter. For the occasion of the blind building, The Buckmaster's nephew, Beef, joined us. Beef was, and still is, my best friend and fishing companion.

THE FISH OF A THOUSAND CASTS

When he wasn't busy chasing girls, Beef tried to be a Junior Buckmaster. At that time Beef was a little rotund and lacked success in both girl chasing and deer hunting. As you get to know Beef, you'll begin to understand why. I'm not saying that to insult Beef's intelligence, oh no! He does a good enough job of that on his own! While most other people put sports or band symbols on their High School class rings, Beef chose a big buck to signify his futility at deer hunting. He may not be the brightest bulb in the box sometimes, but his futility is a great source of amusement for Wally and I! None the less, I love him like a brother...

We were hunting on property that belonged to Beef's other uncle so even though I wasn't really enthused about my location, I was in no position to argue. The Buckmaster and Beef had choice spots that overlooked well-traveled trails. I, on the other hand, was relegated to a briar patch. Oh well, I was the rookie and beggars can't be choosers.

The other two started throwing together clumps of logs and canvas to make their blinds... very unimpressive. Unlike Beef's ugly pile of leaves, my blind was going to be a thing of beauty. My father, who claims to be the reincarnation of a great Indian chief, had taught me how to manufacture a number of outdoor shelters. Throwing sticks and leaves together just wasn't good enough. After countless hours of hard work, I finished construction on a blind that sort of resembled an Iroquois longhouse. My Dad, Chief Squatting Bear as I've nicknamed him, would have been proud. I'd have shown it to him, but The Chief and my mother were flitting about the Bahamas at the time.

Once the blinds were built, The Buckmaster broke out his jug of "Secret Deer Attractor". The attractor was nothing more than ammonia mixed with apple cider. I didn't want to question the Master's hunting methods, so as instructed, I sprinkled a little bit of the formula around the area I was going to hunt.

Needless to say, I didn't want to meet the buck that was attracted to that noxious concoction in a dark alley!

The anticipation of opening day was becoming too much for me to take. As I drifted off in peaceful slumber each night, visions of a monster buck standing before me took shape. It would gracefully appear in the distance and drift toward my blind like a magnificent poltergeist. I was giddy at the thought of aiming the gun and dropping the antlered giant with a precise, single shot. I'd fantasize about my picture on the front page of the local newspaper with a headline that read: *LOCAL MAN BAGS RECORD BUCK!* Events like that are front-page material in Hillsdale County and I was going to be a celebrity.

After all the prerequisite stuff like sighting in the gun, checking the blinds, and listening to the Buckmaster's lectures, opening day finally arrived. We left his house at 4:00am and then spent the next hour trying to get Beef out of bed. Once Beef, who was showing the effects of a night of girl chasing, was dumped into the back of the truck we were on our way.

It was still dark when I settled into my blind and tried to follow the expert advice that The Buckmaster had given me: shut up, sit down, and don't move. As the sun rose, I could hear the distant, thunderous, sound of gunshots. Every once and awhile I'd see a doe sprint across the cornfield and into a swamp that bordered the backside of the property. I could see The Buckmaster as he patiently scanned the cornfield and fencerow, never moving, yet scanning everything. Beef, on the otherhand, was leaning against a tree in a deep sleep. A couple of times I thought I heard a buck grunt but then realized that it was only his snoring.

The serenity of the wild started to get to me and I was beginning to drift off myself when . . .

THUNK! I felt something hit the top of my head. When I looked up, there was a red squirrel directly above me chewing acorns and dropping the shells . . . right on my head. The only sound in the woods was his constant gnawing, cracking, and finally, the dropping of the acorn. *Chisel Chisel Crack! . . . Thunk! Chisel, Chisel, Crack . . . Thunk!*

The morning grew longer and the sun was right overhead. I'd yet to have a buck venture my way and the distant gunshots were becoming less and less. I would've been concerned that I wasn't going to get my buck but I was too preoccupied with the torture that I was enduring at the time. *Chisel, Chisel, Crack! Thunk!* Just when I thought the squirrel was done eating, he'd start up again. *Thunk!*

Snap! Wait a minute . . . something was walking toward my area. I could make out the shape. It was a deer! I couldn't see if there were horns yet but I hoped that it would keep coming closer. The squirrel, meanwhile, had become more intense in his dropping of acorns. *Thunk! Thunk! Thunk!*

Despite the actions of the demon squirrel, time was moving in slow motion and I could see the deer much clearer now. It had horns! I counted six points and my heart began to race. *Thunk!* I slowly raised my head and glared at the squirrel who, in turn, glared back and flashed me a squirrel's version of an obscene gesture. *Thunk!* The deer was now in range. *Thunk!* I slowly stood up and raised the gun to my shoulder. *Thunk!* I took aim and . . . *BOOM! BOOM! BOOM!*

The rapid succession of gunshots startled everyone! The Buckmaster came running down the trail. Beef leaped into the air, yelled something about an angry father and took off running in the opposite direction. That in its self wasn't unusual. Angry fathers protecting their daughters' virtue is so common in Beef's world that he's become a light sleeper . . . and a bit paranoid. The woods fell hauntingly silent and I stood motionless; lost in the sanctity and silence of the moment.

"Did you get him?" The Buckmaster asked when he finally got to my blind. He was looking out over the cornfield.

I looked up at the still smoldering branches above my head and replied, "I don't think so... maybe if I was using buckshot I'd have had a chance. *It's impossible to hit something that small with a slug.*"

Not only had I let the master down and allowed the buck of my dreams to get away, somewhere in the woods that damn squirrel was laughing his tail off at the way he'd narrowly escaped the wrath of this hunter. Beef finally stopped running.

"Hey! *How come I'm running?*" He shouted from the top of the trail. "Must've had a nightmare."

I really haven't been hunting much since then. Although I may not be much of a hunter, I've got to confess that I LOVE hunting season. When everyone else is out in the woods and I have the Steelhead and the rivers all to myself, *I really love hunting season.*

Taking The Plunge

After a day on the Grand River recently, the thought crossed my mind that we fishermen and women seem to take for granted the everyday occurrence of falling in the water. The Plunge, as I often refer to it, is a delightful way to break up the monotony of a slow day on the water. As I plodded my river soaked body back to my vehicle, I stopped to reflect on the art of executing a good plunge.

Many individuals in the fishing community just aren't aware that the plunge is a mandatory event and are under the illusion that it will never happen to them. Nothing could be further from the truth. At some point in time you'll be given the opportunity for plunging and how you execute it will determine your moxie in the eyes of your fellow anglers. My trusted companions, Wally and Beef, have casually referred to me as an expert when it comes to taking the plunge. During our many adventures together, I usually reaffirm my expertise in the plunging field by demonstrating my skills numerous times. As Wally puts it, "No one can get wet like 'Hutch'!"

First and foremost, technique and presentation are the

most important aspects to getting wet. Where many go wrong is the technique with which they attempt the plunge. Often, the first reaction is to flail about and resemble a wounded duck. This only draws attention to yourself and is especially embarrassing if you're on a river where there are many spectators.

The second reaction is to unleash a stream of words that are unprintable in this "family oriented" book. I've seen guys take the plunge and then follow it up by unleashing a torrent of profanity so severe that it would offend most HBO programmers AND stand up comedians.

While both of those are natural reactions during and after a plunge, they only take away from the artistic value that one can accomplish when attempting such a feat.

A simple plunge can be approached in this way: if you're wading down stream and a rock with a penchant for mischief decides to get in your path, you engage in the most common form of plunge, "The Headfirst Dive". As the name implies, you fall forward and submerge into the river headfirst. When you surface is where the artistic portion of the plunge comes into play. Ignore the urge to flail about and simply stand back up, look around to those fishing near you and say "Boy, waters a little brisk this morning isn't it?" and make a cast as if nothing happened. This gives the illusion that you are unaffected by the event that took place and also disarms those around you. Once disarmed, your fellow anglers may have a hard time finding cute and cocky comments with which to torment you. Truth be known, most of us have taken the plunge at one time or another and therefore cautiously observe others who slip and fall. If you act crazy and lack imagination, then you open yourself up to endless ridicule. If you attempt a plunge with style and grace, AND act nonchalant afterwards, all you may get is a simple nod of the head acknowledging that, indeed, the water IS cold. The flailing and profanity is what draws attention, not the plunge itself. Most people won't even notice a graceful quiet plunge thus sparing you from creating a spectacle of yourself. Be wary if you have friends like Wally and Beef. Even if you successfully perform a "Headfirst Dive", they'll no doubt feel obligated to draw attention to it by shouting, "Hey! Did you see that?" or "Where's the video camera when you really need it?" Friends like this must be silenced as soon as you exit the water. Physical violence is usually sufficient enough and draws attention to the squabbling and away from the plunge itself.

"The Swan Dive" and " The Dog Paddle" are two more common plunges. "The Swan Dive" usually is negotiated from a dock or boat. This technique occurs when you trip over your tackle box or cooler and launch yourself off of a dock into the pond your fishing. If you're in a boat, "The Swan Dive" can be implemented when your fishing partner inadvertently steps on the throttle of the trolling motor thereby sending you into the air and, finally, into the water. The easiest way to recover from this type of plunge is to swim around for awhile and "pretend" to be getting a little relief from the summer heat (note: this kind of behavior during the cold months may get you some time in a psychiatric ward). Again, physical violence is called for if "The Swan Dive" is caused by a reckless fishing partner whose name happens to be Beef.

"The Dog Paddle" is effective when you're wading in a river and you step into an unknown hole. This takes quick reflexes. At the same instance you feel yourself slipping under, place your hands in front of you and "Dog Paddle" across the hole. Make sure to keep your head above water or else you will revert to a bad version of "The Headfirst Dive". A successful "Dog Paddle" is a thing of beauty. As with "The Headfirst Dive", resist the urge to flail about.

While the main goal is to not draw attention to ones self, the art of the plunge has not gone unnoticed by those in the sporting goods sector. On the market we now have fishing vests that inflate when a plunging angler pulls a string. If said angler steps into a deep hole, he simply pulls the ripcord and the vest inflates keeping him buoyant. With today's digital technology, I fully expect to see a vest on the market that not only inflates but also plays a high quality MP3 version of "Row Row Row Your Boat" when activated. The cocky angler won't even allow a good plunge to interrupt his fishing. He'll simply keep casting while he gently bobs down river, all the while giving everyone he passes a smug look. Wally and Beef point out these vests every time we get a new sporting goods catalog, but I refuse to succumb to technology. A plunge is a plunge and any attempts to side step a plunge will surely upset the fishing gods and may throw the entire balance of nature out of whack!

Like an earthquake, you can't predict when a plunge is coming. When your number's up, it hits you and you have to react with lightening fast reflexes. Case in point: last summer as Beef and I were launching my boat into Lake Michigan at 5:00am, a plunge appeared on the horizon and I was powerless to stop it. After backing the boat into the launch site, I walked out onto the dock and had to step from the dock to the bumper of my truck so I could unhook the tow cable from the front of the boat... a task I'd performed numerous times.

"The trailers too far from the dock!" Beef advised as I was getting ready to step off. "Maybe I should pull it out and try to back in closer!"

"Naw... it's not that far," I said. "I can reach it! We're wasting valuable time here!"

Apparently Beef was right, a rare occurrence, and the distance from the dock to my bumper was a lot farther than usual. When I "hopped" out to my bumper, my left foot slipped out from under me. With cat like quickness I reached out for the dock with my right foot. As my left foot was still airborne, my right foot landed on the edge of the dock and due to some slippery substance was then propelled into the air. The force of all this caused me to spin in mid air and crash down into the water, or should I say, six inches of water with a solid concrete bottom. Instead of lying there in excruciating pain, I jumped to my feet, silenced Beef with a calculated glare and looked to see if any of the other people launching boats had witnessed what happened. I adjusted my hat, unhooked the boat, and continued with my launching duties. To hear Beef describe the incident, it appears that this all happened within a milli-second but I can assure you that the time it took from first slip to actual impact was as long as it takes to watch grass grow. Ignoring his childish laughter and smart comments we started out of the harbor. As soon as we were a safe distance from the dock, I handed Beef the controls of the boat and curled my crushed body into a fetal position inside the cabin.

"That was absolutely classic!" My trusted companion said after he'd controlled his laughter, "You gonna live or do you want to wimp out and go back home?"

"Hell no, that didn't hurt much. What's a few broken bones anyway?" I valiantly replied. "By the way, did anyone see me fall?"

"Nope, nobody saw a thing," Beef answered. "Although I'm shocked that everyone didn't look when you bounced off the concrete... it was a pretty loud smack!"

Damn right it was loud, and it hurt like hell! But the point was lost on my ignorant friend. *No one saw a thing!*

I sat back up and painfully smiled. One should always take pride in a successful plunge.

The Not-So-Perfect Storm

There are no greater bodies of water than the Great Lakes. Sure, the oceans and seas may be larger in size and harbor more diverse forms of wild life, but for sheer greatness how do they compare to the Great Lakes? Well, the answer is they don't. There's no scientific fact behind that statement and I'll admit that it's rather biased. The simple truth is that the oceans and seas can't compare to the Great Lakes because they don't border Michigan and I'm a Michigander through and through.

The Great Lakes call out to us sportsmen with a sirens song that's more alluring than anything you've read about in books of mythology or fairy tales. They rustle us from our warm beds at ludicrous hours of the morning to take part in the pursuit of feisty aquatic species like Salmon and Steelhead. They enrage loved ones as they force us to turn our backs on household chores in favor of said aquatic species. And, certainly, they are loved by bankers and lending companies who supply us the cash to purchase the needed equipment required in chasing the above mentioned aquatic species.

THE FISH OF A THOUSAND CASTS

Michigan, Superior, Erie, Ontario and Huron: the names of these powerful inland seas evoke excitement at mere mention. Their following is many as Michigan alone has one of the largest concentrations of registered boaters in the United States. Songs have been written about them and their gentle, rolling waters provide the perfect get away from the rigors and stress of everyday life.

They are to be respected though. For all their majesty and splendor, the Great Lakes are powerful... and fickle.

Yes, their power is to be appreciated. I may have taken their power for granted in the past, but I have full appreciation for them now. Perhaps it was wisdom creeping into my life. Perhaps it was simply reflecting on my youthful ideals. Better yet, perhaps it was the fact that an enormous wall of water was making its way toward me as I stood on the deck of my boat! If one can't gain respect from impending doom then I don't know what will do it. Not that I required this kind of lesson in respect, mind you. Oh no, a simple reminder was all that was needed—*not a full blown Tsunami for crying out loud!* But alas, time was frozen and my good friend Wally and I were paralyzed with fear as a mammoth mass of H2O surged ever closer to the boat.

But, I would be doing a great disservice if I picked up the story here. So, to keep the record straight and make crystal clear the events leading up to this point, I'll rewind to the beginning...

In the recent past, the song of the Great Lakes lulled me into buying a boat. I had the boat outfitted with down riggers, fish finders, and all those other items needed for big lake fishing. My boat, the "Licensed to Kill", is a fine boat and handles Lake Michigan with relative ease. Like all new boat owners, I had this insatiable desire to show it off. My best friend Beef helped me outfit it and joins me every time I take it out, so he didn't count when it came to showing off. My other associate, Wally, had yet to see the boat and had to be content with my phone reports and updates of recent fishing trips.

Wally and I live a couple hours apart and our fishing time together has to be set up well in advance. We're both busy people who have to deal with these annoying and time consuming things called "jobs". Due to these "jobs", our fishing time is limited. I kept prodding Wally to get up to my place for a day on the boat, but we couldn't narrow down a date. Both of us had recently come under siege from the terrorist acts of a nefarious organization called Wilderness Intervention For Everyman, or W.I.F.E. for short.

This was back in the "dark times" when I was married and my W.I.F.E. had developed a habit of planning family and quiet time, oddly enough, on weekends. Her idea of "family time" involved dragging me to a mall and forcing me to stare at the floor for hours on end while she tried on EVERY article of clothing that was within seeing distance . . . and her eyesight was quite good! If I'd complain, then that's where the "quiet time" came into play. My W.I.F.E. wasn't content to just take her young daughter shopping; she liked to have me there. On occasion, I'd worked out an arrangement where I went fishing and my wallet accompanied her. This had worked in the past because, as she put it, "she still felt close to me". Wally's W.I.F.E., on the other hand, doesn't like me much so there is a lot of hair raising and nail biting when my name is even mentioned! In addition, she likes to plan all kinds of household chores that can only be done on the weekends that he's planning to fish with me.

Despite the evil efforts of W.I.F.E., we were able to confirm a day when Wally would join me on the boat.

The day before Wally's inaugural trip was a banner day. Beef and I each boated our limit of Salmon and Steelhead. The lake was almost glass calm and there wasn't a cloud in the sky. The fishing certainly looked good for the next day. Beef was a little upset because prior commitments with his

THE FISH OF A THOUSAND CASTS

lady friend of the week would prohibit him from joining us. I told him that as long as he stayed single he was immune from the actions of W.I.F.E. and that whatever plans he had could easily be re-arranged to accommodate some fishing. Beef mumbled something about "hormones" and I dropped the subject. No need to further irrate my best friend.

As we were heading back into the port of Grand Haven, I noticed a dark haze appear on the horizon. The haze moved in very quickly and soon after we'd trailered the boat the rumble of thunder was heard.

"If this keeps up, you won't be going out tomorrow," Beef said.

"Aw, this isn't going to last," I said. "The lake will be fine tomorrow."

The rain was falling in a torrential down pour when Wally and I hitched up the boat the next morning. Prior to leaving the house, I had turned on the weather channel and the radar showed that most of the storms were way north of us and it appeared that the weather would be breaking soon. Since Wally had made the trip up to my house, we decided to give it a go. Wally's eldest offspring, Wally Jr., was going out with us. Wally Jr. was fast into his training of being an outdoorsman and at the age of four was ready to be introduced to the big lake fishing experience.

As we launched the boat, the marine weather channel indicated that a small craft advisory was in effect for Lake Michigan.

"What does that mean to us?" Wally asked.

"It means that small boats shouldn't go out," I replied. "But, as you can see, this boat is 23 feet... it's not small!"

It's about one mile from the boat launch to the actual entrance of the lake. We were motoring down the Grand River and up on a hill, over looking the harbor, stood a giant cross. The cross wasn't there the day before and with it being Sunday and all, I didn't see it as an omen of things to come. As usual, I was blind to the obvious...

The boat started to rock as we approached the pier heads that mark the entrance to Lake Michigan. There were some waves, but at a distance, they appeared to be fishable. We exited the harbor and it soon became apparent that the "small craft" advisory was in effect for all boats that were of less size than the Edmund Fitzgerald! Wally gave me a curious look when I announced that the waves were "navigable" and told his son to hang on for dear life. He knew the look of a crazed boat owner when he saw one and I could easily be classified as that. Mother Nature wasn't about to make me chicken out. Nope, it was going to take more than a few waves to make me turn tail. To lighten the mood, I started singing:

"Just sit right back and you'll hear a tale..."

You know the rest of the song so I won't go into details. My poor attempts at humor didn't lighten Wally's apprehensions.

Funny thing about Mother Nature, she certainly can tell when someone is being belligerent and she had plenty more in store for this charter.

The waves were too high for me to show off how fast the boat could go so we chugged along at a low speed until we reached the seventy-foot depths. Beef and I had killed the Salmon the day before in this spot and I used my GPS to guide us back today. Immediately, the fish finder marked a bunch of Salmon below the boat. That made Wally forget about his tension and the day started to get interesting.

My first task was to set up the downriggers; a task that was fairly difficult because I had to cling to the railing of the boat so the waves wouldn't knock me in the water. With one hand on the railing and the other operating the rigger, it was quite nerve racking to say the least. I'm glad I only had two down riggers to set. Once that task was accomplished, we were enjoying a nice, rocky, ride on the lake.

THE FISH OF A THOUSAND CASTS

It's hard to describe what it's like trolling in the kind of waves that we were but I'll give it a try. First, you're only going about two miles an hour so traveling at that speed doesn't give you an opportunity to cut through the waves. Instead, they carry you in the same fashion that they pass underneath you. I was attempting to go with the waves so the back end of the boat would slowly rise and dip down as the front end of the boat would rise. Up, down, up, down, slowly rising and falling, up, down, up, down ...

"Daddy, I don't feel good," said Wally Jr.

"Urp!" was his father's reply.

I, myself, would've had a snappy comment but I was too busy trying to keep all *my* breakfast items within me. It wasn't all bad though, the rain had stopped awhile back and all we had to contend with were the waves. Wally was steering the boat and I, like a good guide, was monitoring the rods for some sign of action.

I'd stare intently at one rod and then shift my attention to the other. Due to having my focus pointed squarely on the fishing rods, I didn't notice any of the conditions around the boat.

Just as I was switching my gaze from one rod to the other, something caught the corner of my eye and I glanced to check it out.

Black ... pure black is the best way to describe the ominous curtain that was bearing down on the boat. The before mentioned wall of water was making it's way toward us and I was frozen with fear. Wally had also become aware of the omnipresent liquid threat that was swiftly moving in our direction.

There was, of course, the obligatory utterance of profanity that was crude and explicit, yet it summed up the whole of the situation completely. Had Wally and I not been paralyzed with fear, we might've taken exception to the fact that such an expletive was unleashed from the mouth of a four year old child. In fact, I probably would've given the kid a pat on the back had the situation been any different. Finally, I was the first to snap out of the fear induced hypnosis.

"You might wanna push the throttle down and get us the hell outta here!" I screamed. It was no time to remain calm!

Wally had us at full throttle when the wall overtook us. As soon as it hit, a torrential down pour erupted. The wall picked the boat up and carried us a few feet before dropping it back down. The waves, which had been an uncomfortable 3 to 5 feet high, were now a panic inducing 7 to 10 feet high! Wally instructed his son to get in the cabin of the boat and I assumed control of the vessel. Wally decided his best bet was to join his son in the cabin. Every now and then, he'd come out to see if I needed any assistance.

The rain was falling so hard that I couldn't see a thing. I used the GPS to stay in a direction that would head us toward shore and just as I was starting to calm down because I had things under control, Mother Nature decided to unleash her grand finale.

If you've never smelled the scent of ozone in the air, then you're really not missing anything. The first bolt of lightening hit so close that I swear I heard the explosion of thunder before I saw the actual blinding bolt. When it hits so close that your hair stands up, you have cause for alarm. To say that I was alarmed is woefully understated. Full blown, God fearing panic is a little more accurate.

Dodging lightening bolts and jumping waves with such form that Evel Keneval would be envious, we were actually able to outrun the storm. In an instant, I jumped the last wave with the prop screaming out of the water and emerged from rain induced darkness into calmer waves and precipitation free air just outside the harbor.

Do you think I slowed down? *Heck no!* I ignored every basic speed law inside that harbor and tore full bore toward the boat launch. The coast guard wasn't going to do anything because I wasn't the only one violating the no wake rules. Boat after boat emerged from the dark wall of blackness and kept racing into the harbor.

As one boat was passing me, its passengers were waving and pointing behind my boat. I slowly turned my attention to the rear of the boat and noticed what they were referring to. Both of my downrigger balls were skipping across the top of the water behind the boat; no small feat, since they were both 10 pounds of solid lead—but that wasn't the disturbing part. At the same time that Wally had put the boat at full throttle, reeling in the downriggers and the rods was the last thing on our minds. As a result, a rather small salmon that decided to take a bite of breakfast was instead taken for the ride of his life. I couldn't help but feel sorry as I watched the fish skipping across the top of the water while I was running full tilt toward the boat launch. The good thing about it was that I didn't have to filet the fish—the momentum of the high-speed ride pretty much took care of that! Wally Jr. started crying.

"What's the matter, son?" Wally asked. "Did that scare you?"

"No!" his son wailed.

"Then why are you crying?" Wally questioned.

"I didn't get to catch a fish!" the young boy sobbed. We definitely had another sportsman in the making.

We quickly loaded the boat on the trailer and sat in my Explorer as the black wall passed over the parking lot and unleashed the terror we had narrowly escaped. I was enlightened by my newfound respect for the Great Lakes and the power that they can produce in the blink of an eye.

Wally actually started laughing over the whole thing and I quickly joined in.

"I told you that boat could handle anything!" I said between fits of laughter.

"Yeah . . . and we didn't get skunked!" Wally replied.

Then he realized exactly what his son had exclaimed out on the lake and his laughter stopped.

"You better not let your mother hear that kind of thing buster," Wally scolded. "If she does, we're both dead!"

A few weeks later, as the season was winding down, I knew that the lake was going to be glass calm so I invited Wally and the boy for another trip. Wally's wife answered the phone and tried to keep her composure as she admonished me for being a bad influence on her husband . . . and son. Apparently, the boy *did* repeat his colorful phrase and guess who was blamed for teaching him such expressions?

I'm now the poster child for W.I.F.E's new "This could happen to your child" campaign. Hmmm . . . Go figure!

The Pine River Plunge

At first I thought it was all just a bad dream, but reality set in and there I was, dragging a canoe down a snow covered bank in mid February. The plan was to spend two days canoeing the Pine River. A cure, I was told, for cabin fever. The motley assortment of would be canoeists was made up of The Chief, Beef, Wally, The Squirrel, and myself.

"Look at all this fresh snow," The Squirrel joyously exclaimed. "Doesn't this make you feel so alive?"

We'd known The Squirrel for years, but he was a relative newcomer to our adventures and had no idea the kind of terrors that awaited him.

Named for his small build and infamous squeaky voice, The Squirrel happened to over hear us planning our attack on the Pine and asked to be considered for enrollment. I offered to let him take my place since I felt the need to pass on this trip due to a "pressing health concern". When it was pointed out by Wally that a pulled wisdom tooth is not a "pressing health concern", I was backed into a corner and coerced into turning in my RSVP for the event. With two canoes, it was mandatory that we round up a fourth fool to accompany us. Despite my efforts to warn the naive young man, The Squirrel was eager to sign up.

On the weekend prior to our trip, I stopped by my parent's house to verify the condition of my canoe, which hadn't seen the light of day in quite awhile. My father, who is an expert in the nuances of canoeism, was immediately inquisitive.

"What are you up to?" he asked.

When I explained the plan to him, he was eager to join in on the excursion. It should be explained that my father has two different personalities. He claims to have vast knowledge of the Indian culture, and more so, demands that everyone refer to him as "The Chief". He'll venture into the woods with nothing more than a hatchet and a bundle of canvas and construct some of the most effective Teepee's known to man. His other personality is that of a globetrotting tourist. It's amazing how the Chief transforms from one personality to the other. One week he's The Chief and the next, he and my Mother are knocking back Margarita's in the Caribbean. I've often wondered what would happen if he crossed personalities by mistake. Just imagine a short, pale, white man running around wearing nothing but an Indian headdress, a pair of Speedo's and flip-flops. This week I caught him in his role as Chief.

"You know, I haven't had the ol' Mad River canoe in the water for quite some time!" The Chief pointed out. "Sounds like it might be fun."

I tried to explain to the Chief that he would need a partner for this event but he wouldn't hear of it.

"The Chief can handle a canoe by himself," he said. "I'll show you boys a thing or two."

There is nothing worse than a smart aleck Chief. Usually, he does end up showing us a thing or two...

The following depiction is designed to warn others to steer clear of this type of adventure.

THE FISH OF A THOUSAND CASTS

FRIDAY, FEBRUARY 16:

The five of us arrived at the Pine River. Heavy snowfall the night before had turned Northern Michigan into "Little Alaska". A recent warm spell had brought quite a bit of rain prior and the river was swollen to its banks. As is the case this time of year a cold front had moved in suddenly and dropped the temperature into the low 20's. Five idiots, high water, 10 feet of snow, and frigid temperatures usually mean trouble. Unfortunately, I was dead on with that assessment.

We dragged the canoes to the river's edge and began loading all of our supplies. The Chief was armed with his hatchet, sleeping bag, and canvas. The rest of us had enough camping equipment to outfit an Arctic expedition and our canoes were packed to the hilt. We launched into the swift current, and thus, the journey began.

It was eight miles to the unloading point. The plan was to canoe to a portion of state land, set up camp for the night, and finish the last three miles on Saturday. Each paddle stroke moved us closer to the unloading point and all I wanted to do was reach that and go back to my favorite winter time place: The Couch.

The Pine is noted for its swift runs and treacherous rapids. Had it been up to me, I'm sure I would have chosen a much more tranquil waterway. I'm not much of a thrill seeker. I like my adventures to not involve bodily harm or, worse yet, cold water dunkings. Both of those options were available at any moment.

We had traveled a quarter mile or so when Beef began to realize that this wasn't the smartest thing he's agreed to.

"What in the heck were we thinking?" Beef stated as if it were an epiphany.

"Oh no, don't even start complaining Mr. Adventure. Where were you when I was trying to explain how crazy this whole idea was?" I replied. "I don't want to hear you whining about it now."

"Dude... I'm cold!" he whined.

Beef was certainly colder after my paddle inadvertently splashed water into his face. You can never trust canoe paddles, you know...

Wally and The Squirrel were just ahead of us in the other canoe. Both were enjoying every minute of the trip and to witness their glee was rather sickening. The Squirrel was snapping pictures of every thing in sight and kept rambling on about feeling alive and being "one with nature". I enjoy being "one with nature" as much as the next guy, but not in February! At this time of year, I only want to be "one with my couch".

We were approaching the first set of rapids. Wally and The Squirrel zipped through with a little difficulty, but none the less, emerged unharmed. The Squirrels high-pitched squeals made their ride seem worse than it was.

"That was awesome!" he squealed.

The Chief, meanwhile, was way ahead of us and navigated the rapids like he was on a leisurely stroll. The rapids almost got him at one point and he nearly had to put his can of firewater down. Beef and I slipped through without major incident and we looked forward to the next two miles of rapid free water.

As evening approached, we found a nice spot along the banks to set up camp. The Chief found a few long poles and, as is his standard operating procedure, soon had white smoke rising from the top of a finely constructed teepee. The rest of us, meanwhile, had gotten the tent stakes into the ground...

A few hours later, we had the tent erected and were getting our sleeping gear set up for the night. The cold would not be an issue as we had the foresight to bring along one of those handy dandy infrared propane heaters. We may have been crazy for being out there in February, but we weren't that crazy!

"Hey Beef," I said. "Hand me the propane tank so I can get this heater going."

"Where is it?" he asked.

"It better be right there in that pile of stuff!" I snapped.

"Uh . . . Wally? You got the tank?" Beef asked . . . weakly.

"No, it was in your canoe . . ." Wally replied.

The resulting commotion and barrage of foul language caused The Chief to take notice and seize the opportunity to impart more of his wisdom upon us.

"You can't forget sticks and logs," he said. "Just look at this nice fire I've got going in here . . . sleep tight!"

After a great deal of groveling, we were able to set up our gear in The Chief's shelter and take advantage of the fire that he had going . . .

SATURDAY, FEBRUARY 17:

The final portion of our journey was under way and, thankfully, the trip hadn't been accompanied by any of our typical *major* catastrophes. Oh sure, we may have forgotten the propane tank and the frying pan for breakfast but that was just maintaining the status quo. Had we remembered the frying pan, we would have forgotten the eggs or something. It's simply a matter of checks and balances when we're on one of our adventures. One thing leads to another. Besides, the frying pan would have been an unnecessary item considering that we didn't have propane to fuel the camp stove.

We made our way toward the biggest and most feared set of rapids on the Pine, which the locals referred to as the "Cookie Tossers". Once we navigated the infamous rapids, we would have smooth sailing to the take out point a couple of miles downstream. To say the least, tension was in the air as our party coasted ever closer. They were still over a mile away but you could sense the fear as it hung over us like a dark cloud.

Speaking of dark clouds, Mother Nature was about to bless us with one of her famous, Michigan lake-effect snowstorms.

Within minutes, the snow was falling with such intensity that visibility was reduced to five feet or so. Beef and I had no idea where the others were. Sometime earlier, Wally and The Squirrel had grown tired of the leisurely pace of the expedition and began paddling faster so as to expedite their trip through the "Cookie Tossers". They were way ahead of us at this point. The Chief, ever the dawdler, got a later start and was quite further behind.

"You think we oughta pull over and wait this snow storm out?" Beef asked.

"You're one of the reasons I'm stuck in this snowstorm and not on my couch watching TV." I said. "Let's just get this over with!"

We edged ever closer to the rapids. The snow and wind were of little consequence as we dwelled on the horrors that awaited us a few hundred yards downstream. We tried to lighten the pressure a little but our efforts were futile. Silence had fallen between us as we strained to hear the roar of the tumbling water ahead. Beef finally broke the silence.

"You think Wally and The Squirrel have made it there yet?"

As if on cue, the hair on the back of our necks stood up. A faint, yet unmistakable, high-pitched sound pierced the cold winter air. It was shrill and had the appeal of fingernails raking a chalkboard. We winced as the sound gained in intensity. Coyotes howled, birds took flight and the sound became much clearer. It was a scream. Wally and The Squirrel had arrived at the rapids.

As suddenly as it appeared, the scream stopped. Beef and I were speechless. He looked back at me with a look of terror that I'll never forget and I shot him a glare that revealed my intentions to deliver great bodily harm to him when this trip was over.

We inched ever closer to our doom and the roar of the rapids was becoming deafening.

Before I go any further, allow me to explain the layout of the rapids. The Pine River is funneled through a small area of rocks and boulders creating a drop of 6 to 8 feet that's spread out over several yards. After the first drop the river forms a large, harmless, pool before reaching the grand finale that tumbles for 25 yards. A large tree hangs over the pool and several sets of scratch marks forever scar the bark of this fine tree. The scratch marks immortalize those foolhardy adventurers that have navigated these rapids since time began. A lasting testament to the effects of testosterone overdose.

Beef and I gripped the sides of the canoe as we entered the first stage of the rapids.

The front of the canoe dropped sharply and I found myself looking down at Beef. Water sprayed all around us and suddenly I was looking up at Beef. More water. We rocked from side to side and the canoe bounced around the rocks like a pinball. There was a great deal of screaming, profanity, and on Beef's part, an embarrassing act of indiscretion. The canoe stopped rocking as we were now in the safety of the pool and . . . *we were still in one piece!*

"We made it through that part and we didn't lose anything!" I announced triumphantly.

"Maybe *you* didn't," Beef grumbled.

We were about to pass under the tree when I noticed several scratch marks that appeared to be quite fresh. The small size of the marks clearly indicated that someone with tiny hands had made them—The Squirrel. Wally has very large hands and the freshly broken branches displayed his attempts to halt their progress through the rapids. The current speed increased dramatically as we passed under the tree. It was almost like someone was pulling back the bands on a slingshot.

Strangely, I felt the presence of something in the tree above me.

"*Heeeeeeeeeeeelp!*" The Squirrel shrieked as he let go of the branch he was clinging to.

"*WHAT THE . . . ?!*" I screamed.

I never got to finish the sentence as The Squirrel landed right on my shoulders and held on to me for dear life. The slingshot was released and the front of the canoe was launched into the next stage of the rapids.

"*Quit messing around back there!*" was the last thing I heard Beef say before he went into a fit of uncontrollable screaming.

The Squirrel's high-pitched squeals were louder than the roar of the rapids. I struggled to get him off me so I could control the canoe. Panic set in.

"GET OFF ME!" I bellowed. "*I CAN"T SEEEEEEEEEEEEEEEEEEEEEE!*"

To describe what happened next in full detail would be impossible. Once the previously mentioned panic set in, the events were a blur and happened too quickly to remember. The Squirrel was clinging to my shoulders when we experimented with the ancient art of levitation. We flew off the seat of the canoe, hovered in mid air for a bit, looked at the water briefly, and finally dropped into the icy cold river. The moment we hit the water, The Squirrel released his death grip on me and attempted to run toward the canoe. His attempts at water walking were noble and would've made Moses proud, but it was only a short time before he succumbed to the icy current and let out the most hair-raising scream I have ever heard in my lifetime. Beef had been thrown high into the air but luckily landed feet first back in the canoe. He was now riding the canoe through the rapids like a surfer dude riding the big one off the beaches of Maui! Beef and the canoe reached the end of the rapids and the force of the sudden slow-down launched him into the cold water. The Squirrel and I had managed to climb onto the rocks near shore. Beef climbed onto a log below the rapids. The canoe continued meandering down stream without it's precious human cargo.

"You guy's alright?" asked a voice from down stream.

It was Wally! He was clinging to a logjam at the end of the pool below us.

"Couldn't be better!" I yelled. "Nothing like being one with nature huh!?"

I won't repeat what The Squirrel's response was.

We stayed there for a little while contemplating the event prior. The Chief, of course, navigated the rapids with little difficulty.

"Looks like you boys showed the ol' Chief a thing or two didn't ya?" he cackled.

We all piled into the Chiefs canoe, caught up with the other two, and eventually found refuge at the take out point. We were loading up the soggy gear when Beef carelessly spoke up.

"Ya know, that wasn't so bad. Next time we'll know how to get through those rapids."

Next time? *NEXT TIME!?* Given the events leading up to and surrounding that statement, there was no way I could ever be held responsible for the actions that followed . . .

Over The River and Through The Woods

I started to wheeze as Wally and I plodded onward through a briar patch. Some imbecile had given Wally directions to a super secret honey-hole and we trampled into the dark woods in search of this Holy Grail.

"How much further?" I gasped. With each step, I could feel the life slipping out of me.

"Shouldn't be too much longer" Wally answered. "He said that once we got to the briar patch, then it wasn't much farther."

"I want to die" I announced. "Just let me lie down..."

"Smoke another cigarette," Wally advised. "You don't see me whining!"

"I'm done smoking" I proclaimed as I lit up. "This is just too much..."

We finally broke free of the briars and stared ahead at another patch of trees. I strained to hear the rush of the stream we were searching for; all I heard was silence.

THE FISH OF A THOUSAND CASTS

"Do you have any idea where the hell we are?" I asked Wally. I leaned against a tree and let my pounding heart settle down.

"Yeah," he said, "we just have to follow this trail right here..."

"What trail?"

"This one right here," he said.

"That's not a trail!" I wheezed. "Unless you're a mouse!"

We continued on. The summer sun was beating down our necks and causing severe dehydration. I envisioned doing great bodily harm to Wally and thought up inventive ways to torture him. We were so far off the beaten track that no one would hear his screams. Was this trek ever going to end?

"I hear water!" Wally finally announced.

"There isn't going to be any fish around after I jump in!" I said.

We broke through the brush and stepped onto the banks of a pristine waterway. The stream was clear and cool. The sun sparkled like little diamonds in the rushing current and the object of our search, a large beaver dam, was just upstream. The pool above the beaver dam was quite large and we saw several fish break the surface. Despite the agonizing journey, it was breathtaking.

Wally and I snuck up to the pool on our hands and knees and began tossing small spinners into the water. The fishing was fantastic as we caught and released brown trout after brown trout. We fished until it was almost dark and made our way back to the vehicle. A mere two hours later, we loaded our gear back into the trunk of Wally's car. I crawled into the backseat, and immediately passed out from exhaustion.

Such is the requirements when you're searching for that "perfect" spot. It has to be hidden and you have to be able to endure great physical hardships in order to reach it.

Sportsmen everywhere have their own little secret spot that only they know about. The exact location is guarded with such secrecy that not even the CIA could find it! It's commonly referred to as a "honey-hole" or "the ol' stand-by". Usually the sportsman visits this spot alone and on the rare occasion that he lets someone accompany him, that individual is blind folded and forced to use their first born as collateral for secrecy.

A friend of Wally's discovered the spot that Wally and I visited. The location was kept secret for many years and the fish hadn't seen a line since Reagan was in office. No longer physically able to make the journey, he passed the torch to Wally. After an intense ritual and blood oath to ensure secrecy, the mad man handed Wally a crude, hand written map. We haven't told anyone about the spot and never will. It's *our* spot now!

Fishermen are the most prevalent owners of secret spots but other sportsmen locate spots as well. Mushroom hunters are notorious for having secret spots. In fact, mushroom hunting is the most competitive of outdoor activities and its practitioners can get down right vicious in keeping their harvest grounds under wraps. I once went mushroom hunting with The Buckmaster and he turned into a completely different person once we entered the woods. Like all mushroom hunters, The Buckmaster was consumed with the paranoia that someone was following him.

"Keep watching behind you," he said. "Did you see that guy eyeballing us as we got out of the truck?"

"I think he was looking at your truck," I said. "It isn't everyday that you see deer horns for a hood ornament."

"He wasn't looking at the truck!" The Buckmaster argued. "He watched us go up the trail and I'll bet he's following us right now! I'm gonna get us off the trail and try to cover our tracks..."

Which he did. We wandered way out of the way in an attempt to throw off the mystery person who *wasn't* following us. I didn't have anything better to do and was just along

THE FISH OF A THOUSAND CASTS

for the ride. I don't even like mushrooms! I just wanted a little fresh air. The actions of The Buckmaster seemed ludicrous but I wasn't about to question the tactics of a paranoid mushroom hunter! When we finally got to his "ol' stand by", he disarmed all the numerous booby traps he'd set up and we filled our buckets with morels.

"Watch out for that bear trap over there!" he said when I wandered toward another patch of fungi.

In all outdoor conversations, you hear someone brag about their secret spot. There's the pheasant hunter that discovered a meadow that's loaded with huge birds. There's the deer hunter who knows of a swamp that's nick named "The Bog of Bucks" and you can't forget about the fisherman that fills his freezer with slab bluegills from a hidden farm pond. Secret spots are everywhere.

The basic requirement for a secret spot is that it has to be in a location that is extremely difficult to get to. It has to be a test of physical endurance and can't be visited with regularity. I have some spots that I haven't been to in years. Not for lack of time, mind you, I just don't feel like putting myself through a rigorous workout in hiking to them!

They have to be so well hidden that if anyone does find it, then they're entitled to stake partial claim of the spot. The path you choose to follow should take you on a journey of epic proportions and be as painful as possible. Sacrifice and bloodshed are mandatory during the pilgrimage and you never leave any clues as to your whereabouts.

In today's high tech digital age, sportsmen have gravitated to the use of Global Positioning Systems (GPS) when locating secret spots. They embark on a march that would wear down a platoon of battle hardened marines and then mark their exact longitude and latitude on the GPS. Somewhere, there has to be a computer savvy outdoorsman that's capable of hacking into a satellite memory bank and extracting vital logistics. That could be the drawback to using a GPS and is the main reason why I stick to the old tried and true: memory. I can just imagine a covert group of sportsmen who use such espionage in pirating secret spots.

"Benny Johnson's been bragging about a spot that's loaded with brookies" Spy # 1 would say. "He's on his way there right now..."

"No problem!" answers Spy # 2. "I'll simply tap into this communications satellite and get a fix on Benny's GPS signal. There we go... he's in the Freak Em Out Forest heading due east toward Creepy Creek."

"Can you mark it on a map?" asks Spy # 1.

"Yep... I'll store it in the information bank and we'll be knee deep in brook trout in no time!"

The old timers never had access to this technology, which is the sole reason why their spots have never been discovered. The easiest way to find such locations is by chumming up with one of those old timers. Every old timer has a secret spot and once they're unable to get there anymore, they might be willing to reveal its location to the right person. I've shoveled snow, mowed lawns, ran errands and sat through countless tales of old in order to be handed the map to a secret spot. Old timers just don't pass that information on to anyone; you have to prove yourself worthy. The rewards of such perseverance far out-way all the mundane tasks you have to do to prove yourself! The spot will always be productive.

I once knew this elderly gentleman who told me about a spot for monster bluegill. He simply called it his "honey-hole" and never gave a hint to its location.

"That damn Horace Palmer has been trying to get it out of me for years," the gentleman once said, "once you get a honey hole, you gotta cover your rear end cuz someone's always's trying to wrestle it out of you!"

I patiently waited two long years listening to his tales of yesteryear, mowing his lawn, and getting his groceries be-

THE FISH OF A THOUSAND CASTS

fore he felt I was worthy enough to be handed the knowledge of his spot.

One day during one of his lengthy tales, he felt that I was responsible enough to take hold of his secret spot. As he finished telling me a story that he'd told a hundred times, he brought up the subject of the "honey-hole".

"The time has come," he said. "You are worthy."

He got up from his kitchen table and walked over to the windows. He closed every blind in the house and locked all the doors before speaking in hushed tones.

"Now... before I tell you this," he whispered. "You have to sign, in blood, your vow to keep it a secret."

"In blood?" I asked weakly. "It's just bluegill."

"They ain't just bluegill!" He hissed. "*These are BLUEGILL!* There's a BIG difference, you know."

"But blood seems a little excessive," I said. "What if I just agree to sign over my first born like everyone else does!"

"That comes later," he said. "First you sign in blood... you don't think these spots are revealed without certain provisions do you?"

I shook my head. "Good," he said. "Now sign!"

I pricked my finger with a safety pin and signed my name to a tattered piece of paper, which the old man quickly sealed in an envelope. He placed the envelope in a rusty lock box and sat back down at the table. I felt as uncomfortable as a prospective homeowner sitting across from a banker.

What followed was a sadistic ritual that would make Genghis Khan green with envy. I agreed to give up my first born should I reveal the honey-hole's location and promised not to over-harvest the spot. Catch and release was encouraged so as to keep the spot productive long after I retired to the after life. One of the rewards in having a secret spot is maintaining it for future generations. Even if you choose to take the knowledge to your grave, the next person who endures the torturous journey and stumbles upon it should be able to enjoy all it's glory!

I left the old man's house with a hand written map and his next door neighbor, Mr. Horace Palmer, glared at me as I walked up the side walk. He knew I had the location of the honey-hole.

The very next day, I spent four hours navigating thorn bushes, wading through streams and climbing trees before I reached the old man's secret spot. It was a small pond and was loaded with some of the finest bluegill ever seen by man. It may seem like a great ordeal just to catch a few bluegills but these were MY bluegill now! Taking squatters rights over such a spot is the reward for all the suffering. I made sure that I cleaned up any evidence of my activities and took a different way back to my vehicle. I've kept its location secret as I promised I would. I'm very selfish and am really not in the mood to share my bluegill with anyone.

If someone works hard and finds the spot on their own, I'm OK with that. I can't keep vigil over it 24 hours a day, seven days a week and it is located in a public domain. The person who finds it will just have to be careful of all the booby traps I've set, that's all!

Now, if you prove yourself worthy, I might be inclined to let you in on its location. All you have to do is sign in blood right here on the dotted line. Oh yeah, and we can't forget about your first born either...

Moonlight Madness

Darkness. Some people have a paralyzing fear of it. Heck, some people are so consumed with darkness that they'll spend every waking moment of their existence trying to avoid it... but not me. I love the night.

I have my apprehensions about the dark, don't get me wrong, but I simply am not afraid of darkness. It's the things that live *in* the darkness that scares the hell out of me! I'm not talking about animals, oh no. I'm referring to things of another nature: *killers!* Axe murderers, machete massacres, or chainsaw Charlie's... whatever you want to call them, they live in the woods and they only come out at night.

I can read your mind. At this very moment you're deducing that I'm paranoid and, worse yet, assuming that my fear of axe murderers is merely an excuse to cover up an underlying phobia of darkness. That's not the case at all. As I mentioned prior, I just don't feel comfortable with the dangerous characters that prowl the forests at night.

I haven't had this fear all my life. In fact, I never gave it a second thought until I became hooked on those low budget slasher movies that are shown endlessly in late night reruns.

After watching a few of those, you can understand my reluctance to feel at ease after dark, especially in the woods. The plot of these movies is simple: stupid people go in the woods, axe maniac lives in the woods, stupid people meet up with axe slasher, stupid people die.

If you spend as much time in the woods as I do, these movies begin to look like documentaries. You can learn basic survival tips by watching these films closely. For example, if you hear a noise outside your tent in the middle of the night, you don't automatically have to go out and see what it is. People who do can be classified as "stupid". There's a slasher lurking out there! Let him lurk. He's not going to bother coming into the tent. If the killer has to fumble around looking for the zipper of the tent door, then he'll lose the element of surprise. He doesn't want to lose that edge so he'll make strange noises outside in an effort to draw you out.

When I'm wandering in the woods after dark, I'm constantly on the look out for suspicious characters. Is that bush really a bush, or is it a short, fat, machete-wielding-maniac with a pompadour? What about that log lying next to the trail? Is it really a log? Perhaps it's a tall, lanky, strangler with a paper bag over his face.

You think I'm joking? I've survived numerous attacks from assorted butchers due to my keen sense of awareness. Well, that and the fact that I can run really fast!

There was one time that I was supposed to meet Wally, Beef and The Buckmaster in Oscoda for a night of smelt dipping. Somehow, I got distracted by the urge to catch Steelhead and found myself stream hopping on the opposite side of the state. As evening approached, I knew that there was no way that I was going to make it over to Oscoda so I looked for a spot where I could park and sleep in my vehicle. I located the perfect spot along Swan Creek in the Allegan State Game Area. By now, it was well after dark and I was in

THE FISH OF A THOUSAND CASTS

a secluded area surrounded by thousands of trees . . . the perfect spot for lurking killers.

I wasn't tired so I tried to lull myself to sleep by listening to a baseball game on the radio. Didn't work. Being so close to the creek, I wanted to get out and fish. Ignoring my superficial paranoia, I put on my waders and grabbed my rod and lantern from the back of my pick up. To fuel my phobias, lightening flashed overhead as a storm moved in from Lake Michigan.

Do you notice a trend here? If anything jumps out at you by reading these stories, it should be the fact that when I put a fishing pole in my hand the weather is going to be lousy. Steve Hutchins, fishing, and nice weather, *do not go together*. Thunderstorms and/or snowstorms are the normal weather patterns when I take to the outdoors. Right on schedule, a storm was brewing as I made my way down the trail toward the water. I made a mental note of my surroundings, located all the potential killer hiding spots, and made it a point to scan those hiding spots frequently.

The woods along the creek bank were pitch black. So black that my lantern light only lasted a few feet before dying into nothingness. I stood on the side of the creek and saw several things zipping through the water. The next flash of lightening revealed the largest school of Steelhead I'd ever seen in my life! They were everywhere.

Fishing fever took over and my fears were subsided. My hands were shaking as I tied a fly onto my line. The anticipation of all those Steelhead had me giddy. A light rain started to fall and the wind picked up. This was going to be a vicious storm but I didn't care. All I had on my mind were those countless Steelhead. I was getting ready to make my first cast when . . .

ZZZZZZAAAPPP!!!

A lightening bolt hit on the other side of the creek. At some point, I went numb with fear and when I came to, I was racing at full sprint back up the trail.

Suddenly, I heard footsteps behind me! It was a killer! He was hot on my heels! I ran faster but the footsteps kept getting louder and louder. I refused to turn around to look but I knew it was a maniac with a machete behind me. Thank God, my truck was in sight. Just as the footsteps were about to overtake me, I threw all my stuff in the back of the truck and dove in the passenger side door. The killer took one futile swipe with his machete before disappearing into thin air . . .

I tore out of the woods, as a person who just survived such an event should, and sought a comfortable nights sleep at the nearest motel. Killers are notorious for vanishing into thin air once they've missed their opportunity to live up to their namesake. Sometimes, their sheer presence is enough to strike fear into the hearts of wood dwellers.

One such example of this took place in Northern Michigan a few years ago when my father, The Chief, took me and my friend, Smiley, up to the little Manistee River for a weekend of fishing and hunting. We set up camp in a remote access site known as "Bear Track". Smiley and I hiked up and down the river looking for Steelhead while The Chief settled into a makeshift blind in the hope of bagging a nice deer. It was Thanksgiving weekend and the woods were void of other sportsmen.

The emptiness of the forest exuded a peacefulness that mere words can't begin to describe. Overcast skies and a slight warm breeze added to the serenity that we were enjoying. Everything was perfect . . . until it got dark that is.

Once the specter of nightfall settled over the woods, serenity turned to absolute terror. It was pitch black and all we had was one lousy lantern. The artificial light source illuminated a small ten-foot area and that was it. Beyond the light, it was pure blackness.

You couldn't see them, but the killers were lurking.

"Steven," The Chief said, "why don't you grab a few

more logs for the fire?"

"Are you kidding me?" I said. "The logs are clear over there... I'm not going out in that darkness!"

"You spend too much time watching television," The Chief replied.

"I'm not afraid of nothin'," Smiley chuckled. "I'll get 'em."

Smiley is the type of individual who laughs at everything, hence his nickname. His downfall is his failure to acknowledge that evil strangers lurk in the dark woods and love to target people who chuckle at their existence.

"Suit yourself," I said, "I'll notify your mom when I find your corpse!"

Smiley entered the darkness, fumbled around a bit, and returned unharmed with an armful of logs. The killers were trying to lull us into a false sense of security, but I was not so naive.

As it grew later, the wind kicked up quite a bit. The wind shook the tent, and to be honest with you, the sound of it rushing through the many trees was quite relaxing. We were all starting to fall asleep when there was a strange "crack" outside the tent.

"What was that?!" I shouted as I sat up in my sleeping bag.

"That was just the fire," The Chief answered.

"Since when does a fire go for a walk?" I asked.

"Uh... I hear something too," Smiley said *without* chuckling.

"It's probably a raccoon or something," was The Chief's explanation.

SNAP!

"Raccoon hell, that's a killer!"

The hard realization that we were being stalked finally hit Smiley and all I could do was agree with his assessment.

"There is no killer out there!" The Chief stated with a touch of agitation in his voice.

It now sounded like something was being dragged across the ground. No doubt, the killer was bringing in three body bags.

"Get the gun! Get the gun!" I shouted.

"We don't need the gun!" The Chief shouted back. "Besides, it's in the truck."

"Oh great... we're dead for sure!"

The Chief rolled over in his sleeping bag and tried to go to sleep. Smiley and I stared into the darkness toward the tent door, expecting it to open at any moment. Another set of footsteps added into the equation. They weren't as loud and appeared to be made by something very small.

"Wonderful," I said, "now there's a tiny killer out there."

"*There are no killers!*" The Chief shouted before ordering us to go to sleep. "The only killing that's going to happen is if you two sissies don't go to sleep!"

Soon after, the footsteps faded into the breezy night air. There would be no killing tonight, but the damage was done. Smiley and I didn't sleep a wink the rest of the night.

That's what maniacs do best. They strike fear into the hearts of people who enjoy forest activities. You see, if they killed everyone that they came in contact with, no one would venture into the woods. The woods would be crawling with law enforcement officials and certainly no killer wants that.

It was easier in the old days for killers to hone their craft. The woods still had an aura of mystery and if someone didn't return, it was just assumed that a bear ate them.

"Maw, how come pop didn't come home from his camping trip?" a son would ask.

"Bear ate him!" was the mothers reply. No one raised suspicions that dear ol' dad met his fate at the hands of an axe-crazed killer.

Since the onset of those slasher movies that exposed killers to the mainstream, people have grown to fear the evils

THE FISH OF A THOUSAND CASTS

of the forest. The killers know this and now their forte is to scare the pants off of people who set up camps in remote sections of the forest.

Strange footsteps, cracking noises, and dragging sounds indicate the presence of lurking maniacs. They wait until your safely ensconced in your sleeping gear before unleashing their heart-pounding terror. But they're wily, as soon as you peer out of the tent to see what's going on, they vanish into thin air. They don't leave footprints or any other evidence of their visit, but rest assured they're out there.

As long as human beings venture into the woods at night, the killers will always be lurking.

And we'll always be ready to run . . .

Chuck and... DUCK!

I've always had a distant fascination with the sport of fly-fishing. Every month I receive numerous fly-fishing journals and magazines in the mail and admire the grace and eloquence with which the anglers pursue exotic game fish. I've yet to experience the blissful state of perfection that's displayed within these magazines, but I can appreciate the realistic effect of the, obviously, doctored photographs plastered throughout. I'll give them credit, I'm a big fan of special effects and the photographs I refer to are clearly top-notch. Heck, to the untrained eye, they might seem real. I mean, based on my experiences, I've yet to encounter the state of perfection so keenly photographed in those magazines.

Fly-Fishing. The mention of this activity invokes visions of Hemingway conquering brook trout and rainbows on the Upper Peninsula's famed Two Hearted River. It makes you think about the film "A River Runs Through It" where a father and his sons bond and come to understand each other while sharing time on the water fly-fishing. Countless authors

THE FISH OF A THOUSAND CASTS

have song the praises of fly-fishing and those who partake regard this activity with an almost religious sanctity, but if an author was to be commissioned to write of *my* fly-fishing exploits, the only one that could handle this task would be Stephen King. Everything beautiful has a dark side and my contributions to the sport are no exception!

When I first started fishing for Salmon and Steelhead, I was one of the many "spawn tossers" who felt that spawn, or fresh Salmon eggs, was the only way to catch Steelhead. As Steelhead fishing became more mainstream, it was determined that artificial flies were also effective. Armed with this knowledge, some of us were able to dramatically improve our success rates and catch more fish. There's a price to be paid for such success and the price was paid in the cost of a fly. By no strange coincidence, the rise in popularity of Steelhead flies also coincided with an increase in the cost of these precious offerings. Bait shop owners called it "inflation"; the rest of us called it price gouging. Either way, it was a sellers market and the laws of supply and demand dictated the purchase price of these flies. Most of us were selling precious belongings to gather enough money to keep our fly boxes stocked, until Beef and I wandered through a fishing show one winter and stumbled upon a booth where a kindly, elderly gentleman was demonstrating the techniques of fly-tying.

We watched intently as he crafted gorgeous imitations of aquatic insects and it dawned on us that we could save a bundle if we made our own flies. We watched, listened, and wrote notes on a napkin as the demonstrations went on. The old man made it seem so easy. Giddy with our newfound knowledge, we purchased all the necessary supplies and jumped headfirst into the world of fly-tying.

Somehow, the old man was able to put one over on the two individuals who watched so intently. The man was definitely a master of illusion, as the ease with which he assembled such fine looking flies was lost on us! In fact, our first "Flies" looked like something my cat throws up. Speaking of cats, I discovered, via an attempt to reduce costs, that cat hair does not make a suitable substitute for other popular fly-tying materials like squirrel tail. My mother put a moratorium on my experimentation when the family cat began appearing with mysterious bald spots!

But I digress. The horrific appearance of our offerings led us to coin a new name for our creations. Since they didn't resemble an insect in any way, shape, or form, we simply referred to them as "ties". Ties were anything attached to a hook that consisted of fur and feathers. Since we took the liberty to name our creations in such a manner, it would only make sense that the use of such items should be termed "Tie-Flying". The term "Tie-Flying" came out as a verbal mistake one day as I was conversing with a fellow angler on the Manistee River. We were discussing different forms of relaxation and I said that I really find tie flying relaxing. The man looked at me and questioned my oral blunder. I kind of liked the term "Tie-Flying" and it's stuck ever since.

"Tie-Flying" is really just a drop in the bucket in the whole scheme of fly-fishing. There are so many different ways to present artificials to the fish that authors could spend their entire lives researching them. I'm waiting to see the book, *The Complete Fly-Fishing Guide—No Exceptions* on a bookstore shelf. The thing would have to be the size of a dictionary and require the same down payment as a house.

Now that I've brought up the subject of dictionaries, allow me a few moments to point out some catchy fly-fishing terms that most people already know. Easy terms like "Spey" "Double Hand Spey" and "Back Cast". *Back Cast?* How many fishermen use the term "back cast" besides fly fishermen? I've never in my life used that term when spin-fishing. We primitive spin fishermen refer to a cast as . . . *a cast*. The entire steps in executing a cast all fall under the generic term: cast.

THE FISH OF A THOUSAND CASTS

But that's what sets fly-fishing apart from other forms of fishing. There's a name for everything! Kind of like golf...

The effectiveness of flies (or ties) for Salmon, in particular, has caused many people to do things that would border on obscene! Take this for example...

Last fall, I was on the Big Manistee River enjoying a gorgeous September evening. The river was almost void of human presence and I slipped into a nice run that held a bunch of feisty, fresh, Chinook. The stars were out in force, there was very little breeze and the only sound in the river was the hiss of my lantern and the occasional splash of an angry Salmon. It was an angler's paradise to be sure! After a couple hours of relative solitude, I noticed a pair of anglers making their way down the riverbank. They stopped in my lantern light and sat their "stuff" on the ground. Their "stuff" consisted of three fishing rods, a tackle box and two CASES of a cheap, frosty, adult beverage. From the way they staggered down the riverbank, it was apparent that they'd already had their fill of the hops and barley!

"What's goin' on, buddy?" the first angler asked me.

"Oh... not a whole lot." I said. I wasn't in the mood for conversation at that point.

The two tipsy fishermen slid into the river near me and began casting large lures that might've caught a shark... provided you were fishing in the ocean! I continued casting my little peach yarn fly and hooked fish after fish. The drunkards weren't hooking anything and finally got a little fed up.

"What are you doin' that we ain't doin?" the second angler asked. "What you usin'?"

I showed him my little peach yarn fly and explained that it was made to resemble a Salmon egg.

"Looks like a piece of white cotton!" the drunk stated.

"No... it's peach yarn." I explained again. "It's not cotton, and it's not white."

"But, I'll bet white would work . . . wouldn't it?" he asked.

"I suppose white would work," I answered.

That answer was mistake # 1. The intoxicated angler rubbed his chin for a moment and suddenly his eyes lit up in a manner indicating that he'd just come up with a brilliant idea. He wandered back up to his tackle box and I continued fishing. After a few minutes, I heard a strange ripping sound coming from the bank behind me. I was too scared to turn around. The ripping and tearing continued until the drunk staggered back out to the river. He was grinning from ear to ear and proudly displayed the new rig dangling from the end of his rod. It was a large treble hook, about the size of a fist, with a large chunk of white cloth impaled on one of the barbs. Mistake # 2 followed.

"What the hell is that?" I asked, completely unprepared for the answer.

"You said white would work!" the angler proudly stated. "The only white cotton I got is my underwear! So I tore off a chunk and put it on this here hook!"

I was too dumb-founded to reply. The drunk made a cast into the swirling current and with the giant treble hook, snagged a Salmon by the tail. The fish was no doubt surprised by the foreign object in its rear end and leapt from the water, screaming, "What the hell is in my tail? *That looks like freakin' underwear!*"

"Hell Yeah! I got him . . . fish on!" the madman screamed. The fish jumped out of the water again. This time screaming vulgarities and insults at the drunkard. Finally . . . the line broke and the rocket scientist looked at me . . . grinning.

"You're right!" he said, "white does work!"

"Please don't tell anyone . . ." I whispered, as he ripped up the rest of his underwear for bait . . . *waistband included!*

The form of fly-fishing that I practice is the "Chuck n' Duck" method. I'm a writer and my feeble attempts at humor force me to concoct situations and creative nicknames, but I

THE FISH OF A THOUSAND CASTS

can take no credit for the term: "Chuck n' Duck"! If there was ever a term that could appropriately describe my style of fly-fishing, this is it. As it implies, you chuck your tie and then duck, so it won't impale you in the back of the head. The creator of this term obviously failed in the latter portion of the phrase, and hence, coined the name. Most fly anglers in the mid-west practice this technique when fishing for Salmon and Steelhead. The fishes spawning runs can be timed by a direct correlation in the increase of emergency rooms reporting people with hooks in the back of their head. To find out if the runs are on, simply call the local hospital and ask how many people have had to have flies removed from their scalps. If the number is on the rise, then it's safe to assume that the fish are present in decent numbers!

"Chuck n' Duck" is an acquired fishing technique and one that requires patience as well as agility. Beef and I frequently use flies when we're out on the water, but most of the time we still use them on our drift fishing rods. The heresy of that hasn't gone unnoticed by the purists in the fly-fishing community who encourage us to change techniques by shouting helpful hints like, "Get a freakin' clue, would ya!" Those fly guys... they're a wild bunch all right! Beef and I decided, one day, that we needed to expand our horizons and get a better grasp of "Chuckin' and Duckin'".

The best course of action was to book a trip with a guide who's specialized in the art of "Chuck n' Duck". I called an acquaintance of mine that guides on the Pere Marquette River.

"I'd love to help you," the guide said, "but I'm all booked up. Let me make a couple phone calls and see if I can hook you up with someone."

My acquaintance made some calls and booked us with another guide who runs the flies only section of the river out of a drift boat. We were to meet him at "The Blue Bear Lodge".

The guide was waiting for us when Beef and I roared

into the parking lot. I suppose he wondered what he'd gotten himself into when my Explorer screeched to a halt with the radio blasting Judas Priest at full volume. Beef and I got out arguing . . . as we're prone to do when we're stuck in a vehicle for any length of time.

"I think you're way off base on this!" I said. "Bloodsuckers is a much better song than Devil Digger!"

"How can you say that?" Beef shot back. "Devil Digger has better rhythm for head banging!"

"*Bloodsuckers!*" I shouted.

"*Devil Digger!*" Beef shouted back. We were about to take the argument to a physical level when the guide interrupted our debate (which was good for Beef's sake although he'd argue otherwise).

"Please tell me you're not my charter!" the guide pleaded. He buried his face in his hands when we confirmed that we were.

The guide, a Mr. Frederick Palmreel, was well known in the fly-fishing community and an author of numerous articles and books. His vast knowledge of the sport made him a bit arrogant and Beef and I would later refer to him as, Flingin' Freddie.

Flingin' Freddie launched his well-equipped drift boat into the rust colored water of the Pere Marquette and we were on our way. The trip got off to a bit of a rough start. Beef and I were taking a bathroom break as Flingin' Freddie was launching the boat. When we emerged from the public bathroom, Freddie was already drifting down river. He was paddling to beat hell and looked panic stricken when he saw us running towards him. Beef and I finally chased him down and got into the boat. Flingin' Freddie explained that the boat drifted into the current while he was rigging up the rods and, while his paddling may have appeared that he was trying to get away, he was merely trying to bide time until we could catch up to him. Made sense to us . . . like we knew any

THE FISH OF A THOUSAND CASTS

better! It wasn't long before Beef and I picked up where we left off in our argument. Flingin' Freddie grew weary of our lengthy and intelligent conversation.

"Enough with the blood suckin' devil music!" he screamed. "Are you guys here to fish or argue?"

"Both!" Beef answered. "We're good. We can do both at the same time! This boat got a stereo?"

Flingin' Freddie mumbled something that I couldn't make out, but it sounded like some sort of violent insult directed at the acquaintance who'd booked this trip for us.

After drifting a short distance, Freddie ordered Beef to take control of the oars so he could finish rigging up the fly rods. Beef wasn't all that enthused about the task but took over anyway. We passed two anglers who were attempting to wade around a large logjam. Flingin' Freddie gave them some helpful advice as we drifted by.

"Buy a boat you weenies!" Freddie shouted. The two anglers, thankful for the helpful hint, expressed their appreciation by saluting our guide with a popular hand gesture that involves one middle finger. We saw that gesture a lot as the day went on. Flingin' Freddie didn't appear to be too popular with the other anglers on the river. They must've known who he was because they kept calling him by name. Albeit, they used a different adjective in front of it, but it still started with the letter "F"! I was getting tired of drifting; we seemed to be passing up some good water.

"Uh . . . aren't we passing a lot of good holding water?" I asked.

"Who is the guide here?" Flingin' Freddie questioned. I pointed at him. "That's right, and since I'm the guide, I will decide what's good holding water and what's not . . . *got it?*"

That's the thing about guides. Some of them act like you've never held a fishing pole in your life. What Mr. Freddie didn't realize was that I was an outdoor writer as well. Ha! I knew a thing or two about Salmon fishing myself!

"You may be the guide," I said, "but I do know how to fish. And that pool we just drifted over was classic Salmon and Steelhead water. Notice how the tailout is right in front of that logjam? Perfect for cover."

"Yeah... you tell him!" Beef said between oar strokes. "I'm tired of rowing this damn thing!"

"The only reason you're here is to learn how to fish." Flingin' Freddie said. "Now do you want to learn how to fish the right way or do you want to oar this boat all the way to the take out point?"

"He wants to oar!" Beef spoke up.

"Look," I said. "I already know how to fish. I've been drift fishing for years, I just want a few pointers on chuck n' duck."

"Drift fishing is not fishing, so you don't know how to fish." Freddie smugly commented. "If you want to learn how to fish, and there is only one true form of fishing, then shut up and watch the master at work!" With that, he held his arms high in the air and the anchor magically dropped into the river. We settled in a large bend that looked like good holding water.

Flingin' Freddie handed us each a fly rod. He instructed us in the finer points of "Chuck 'n Duck", emphasizing the latter part of the phrase as the most important. I noticed immediately that Freddie's set up was different from ours. His rig consisted of two finely tied egg flies suspended beneath a couple of BB sized split shot sinkers. Beef and I each had some sort of giant fly that roughly resembled an entire skunk tail. It was tied about a foot below a gob of weight that looked, oddly, like an old spark plug.

"Um... How come our flies are different from yours?" I asked. "Aren't these a little big?"

"I don't think mines dead yet!" Beef exclaimed as he dodged an attack by the rabid skunk tail.

"Since you're just learning how to fish the right way, you

THE FISH OF A THOUSAND CASTS

will use practice flies until you get the hang of it." Flingin' Freddie explained.

"But I already know how to fish!" I said. "Give me a real fly!"

"Yeah . . . if he gets one, then I get one too!" Beef added. "How hard can this be?"

Beef arrogantly stripped a few yards of line off the reel, reared back and let the offering fly.

"Is it in past the barb?" Beef asked as I was attempting to dislodge the snarling fly from the back of his head. Flingin' Freddie flashed us one of those "I told you so" looks and gracefully tossed his rig into the pool. Within a few seconds, he was into a fish. The brilliant Steelhead darted around the pool a few times before Freddie had it subdued.

"Net!" Flingin' Freddie demanded. "Now!"

I grabbed the net and our guide masterfully maneuvered the anadromous trout to the boat. He removed the tiny fly from the corner of its mouth and released it back into the pool. Beef and I stripped line off of our reels and, this time, remembered to duck as our grotesque offerings sailed past and plopped on the edge of the pool. We felt nothing. Flingin' Freddie, meanwhile, was into another fish.

"Net!" he demanded again.

"Aren't you supposed to be netting *our* fish?" I questioned. "I'm not paying good money to be your net boy!"

"Yeah, and I didn't pay to oar the boat either!" Beef said.

"You're paying for the privilege of being in the company of my vast knowledge. You are learning to fish!" Flingin' Freddie reported. "Now . . . *NET!*"

And so it went. Beef would row the boat from pool to pool and I was Flingin' Freddie's net boy. We quickly got fed up with this arrangement and waited for an opportunity to turn the tide. Finally, it came.

"Row us over to shore!" Freddie ordered. "I have to go to the bathroom!"

Freddie got out of the boat and disappeared into some bushes. He left his fly box on the front seat.

"Now we'll have some fun!" I told Beef as I opened the box and removed some of the "hot" egg flies that Freddie had been using. Beef and I snickered like little kids. For added insurance, I pinched down the barbs on the flies that Freddie had tied to his line. You can't keep a fish hooked for very long if there isn't a barb!

"What are you two giggling about?" Flingin' Freddie said when he got back to the boat. We told him that we were reminded of a little joke. He eyed us suspiciously.

We dropped anchor at another pool and Freddie, as usual, was the first one to cast. Beef and I cautiously untied the skunk tail flies and attached one of the small egg flies. Flingin' Freddie was into a fish. He was ordering me to get the net when the hook popped free. Beef and I snickered as we tossed our rigs into the pool. I hooked a fish! It was a gorgeous Coho Salmon with silver sides and a classic hooked jaw. I got it under control and maneuvered it toward the boat.

"Net!" I ordered. "Right Now!"

Freddie grabbed the net and began swatting at the fish with it! For all his knowledge, he sure didn't look like he knew how to net a fish.

"What are you doing?" I screamed. "Beef can net a fish better than that!"

Speaking of Beef, he had just hooked a fish. Double header! I continued arguing with Flingin' Freddie while Beef swung his fish, a nice Steelhead, toward the boat. Freddie took another swat at my fish. The line broke.

"You got too anxious," Freddie said. "The fish wasn't ready yet!"

I gnashed my teeth as Beef got his fish close to the boat. Flingin' Freddie began swatting at it with the same end result: broken line.

Beef and I were steaming mad. We glared at our guide,

nodded at each other and the mutiny was under way. Flingin' Freddie's tyrannical reign was over...

We spent the rest of the trip enjoying the beauty of the river and multiple hook ups in each pool we fished. The silence of the woods was occasionally broken by the splashing of hooked fish and the odd, muffled, protest from the front of the boat. As we drifted past numerous anglers on the river, we were greeted with applause and high fives. Maybe it was the courtesy with which we avoided their fishing spots; more likely, it was the sight of Flingin' Freddie seated in the front of the boat with his hands bound behind his back with eight weight fly line and the remnants of a skunk tail fly stuffed in his mouth.

We drifted the last hundred yards to the access site with our arms aching from fighting so many fish. A dozen or so anglers circled the take out point and gave us a standing ovation as we steered the hijacked drift boat toward shore. As I said before, Flingin' Freddie was not a popular character on the Pere Marquette. Better yet, we'd skillfully mastered the art of "Chuck n' Duck", a technique that has served us well during numerous fishing trips. Once we stopped by the emergency room and had all the hooks removed from our scalps, we called it a day.

Courtin' in the K-Zoo Valley

Thunder rumbled in the distance. It was quite a shame because we were having such a wonderful day. Wally, Beef, The Squirrel, and I had been lazily floating down the Kalamazoo River in inner tubes stopping every now and then to catch a few of the planted brown trout that reside in the deeper holes. Fishing wasn't our main priority; it was simply a muggy, sun drenched day and we were enjoying each other's company floating down a cool river like we used to do when we were kids.

My wife and I were back in the area visiting my relatives. Beef, who resides with us in Grand Rapids, was also down for the same reason. Time and space converged perfectly and four old friends were able to spend a day doing nothing except reminiscing about days gone by and consuming the occasional adult beverage. We snagged a few old inner tubes from the local tire shop, packed a few sandwiches, and said a temporary good bye to the rigors of the real world. Believe me, it was nice!

THE FISH OF A THOUSAND CASTS

We were welcomed back to the real world when the thunderclaps intensified.

"Did anyone watch The Weather Channel before we left?" Wally asked.

"Yeah," answered Beef, "it said chance of storms tonight."

"What time is it?" asked The Squirrel, in his infamous high-pitched voice.

"It's 1:30pm," I said, "it's night time somewhere!"

"How far downstream is that bridge we were gonna take out at?" The Squirrel nervously questioned.

The rest of us shrugged our shoulders and kind of guessed that it was a couple of miles at least. Far enough away that we would have to take refuge along the riverbank before the storm hit. The section of the river we chose to tube down was desolate and tree covered. It offered many opportunities to take cover from a storm and we really didn't have to worry about upsetting any landowners since there didn't appear to be any along this stretch. Wally, the past and present boy scout, assumed command of the float trip and determined that the best course of action was to pull up to shore and wait the storm out.

"That big oak tree looks like suitable cover," he announced.

A blinding lightening bolt followed by an intense thunderclap sent us scurrying for the towering oak.

"Good thinking Wally," I said. "I couldn't have picked a better spot myself!"

As the wind started to pick up and the patter of raindrops hit the leaves above us, we flopped onto the ground underneath the tree and used our inner tubes for pillows. Jokes were told, old adventures were recalled, and we poked fun at everything and everyone as Mother Nature unleashed her fury. Other than the occasional muskrat meandering by, we were all alone in those woods. Or so we thought...

"Well, well, well, lookie here Dean," came a strange voice

from behind the tree. The voice, with a pronounced southern drawl, scared the daylights out of us! "Look's like we got us some trespassers!"

Two imposing figures emerged from behind the tree. One was older, maybe 60 years old, and was obviously the father figure. The younger one, Dean, was his son. The father was holding an ancient looking rifle and looked like a refugee from the frontier days. His eyes were sunk into the back of his skull and he had a mangy, unkempt beard that dropped to his chest. His hands were shaking like a smoker in need of nicotine. He was rather short, slightly rotund, and he cradled the gun like a mother with a newborn.

Dean was no where near as creepy looking as his father. He looked like a giant, bearded, eggplant in bib overalls and based on his mannerisms, appeared to have the intelligence of an eggplant. In addition to missing a few a braincells, he was missing most of his teeth.

"Huh, huh, Paw . . . do we git ta kill em?" Dean muttered.

"Naw ya durn idiot," Paw said. "If we go to killin' folks then we'll have that durn sheriff breathin' down our necks and ya know how's I hate dealin' wit the law!"

"What you boys doin' on ma land?"

Wally, since assuming control of the trip, became the designated diplomat. Wally is the sociable type and grew up in an area where folks are friendly. His knack for conversation would be useful in getting us out of this predicament.

"We're terribly sorry sir," he began negotiating. "We were just floating down the river here when the storm hit and we pulled ashore to hide under this fine old oak tree that you have. We certainly didn't realize it was private property and we meant no disrespect in coming here"

"Can I hurt 'em paw?"

"Durn it Dean! Keep yor filthy trap shut when I tells ya! These here look like some fine upstanding gentlemen if ya

THE FISH OF A THOUSAND CASTS

knows what I mean," said Paw with a wink. "Why don't ya come up to the house and wait this storm out."

"Uh . . . alright" was Wally's reply, much to the disagreement of the rest of us.

We followed Paw and Dean up a trail toward a dilapidated old farmhouse. Wally instructed us on how to act and his actions reminded me of Mr. Spock filling in the crew of the Enterprise as they approached a strange new civilization.

"What we have here is a strange life form known as "simple folk". It would be wise to respect their customs and hospitality as they are a people of great pride who are easily insulted when acts of kindness are declined."

Simple folk? Hell, *these were the people that time forgot*! An old hand powered washing machine was on the back porch, there was a hand powered well in the back yard, and of course, there was an outhouse near the corner of a tool shed. This whole scene could've been right out of the sequel to "Deliverance"!

The Squirrel stumbled on our way up the trail and covered himself, from head to toe, in mud.

"Don't worry son, Dean here's got some dry clothes you can put on," Paw said.

Beef was growing agitated.

"Why don't we just say to heck with this storm and get back in the river?" he whispered to me. "The last place I wanna be stuck is here with the Clampetts!"

"You might meet Ellie May," I joked. "Hell, we already met Jethro!"

We walked onto the back porch and Paw took off his rain slicker. He looked down at our hands and then made eye contact with Wally and me.

"I see you two are married," he said.

"Happily!" said Wally.

"Unfortunately!" I sighed.

"But not to each other!" we said in unison, laughing.

"Heh heh heh," Paw cackled. "That's all right, I still might have some use fer ya! Heh heh heh."

Squirrel and Beef followed Dean into the house. Dean told the Squirrel to follow him so he could get some dry clothes on.

"What about them two?" asked Paw. "Is they single?"

"Absolutely! Unattached!" we answered. Paw ran his fingers through his beard and nodded his head in approval.

"Well good . . . them two will do jist fine." he said.

"Jist fine fer what?" was my first thought.

Wally, Beef, and I followed Paw into the house and surveyed the surroundings. The interior of the house mirrored the weathered, ragged appearance of the outside. The kitchen had an old icebox and wood fueled stove. Several cast iron skillets hung on a board above the stove and a little sign that read "Home Is Where The Heart Is" was on display above the sink or, should I say, "wash tub".

A kindly looking, plump woman emerged from a storage closet adjacent to the kitchen area. Her silver tinged hair was packed neatly into a hair net and she was attired in a flowery loose fitting sundress.

"Lord of host Paw!" she exclaimed. "What do we have here?"

"I found em down by the river, Maw . . . I figures two of em oughta make good husband material for Eula and Fannie Sue," Paw replied giving Beef a playful jab to ribs.

Husband material? Ah . . . the picture was clearing up now. Since Wally and I were already married, it became apparent that whatever plot was slowly transpiring, *did not* involve the two of us. As much as I hated being married (if you knew my ex-wife, you'd understand why!), I was glad that I admitted to being so! Our fears immediately ceased and we decided to take advantage of the family hospitality. They did seem like nice "simple folk" after all!

"You boys hungry?" Maw asked. "I'm fixin' to make up

THE FISH OF A THOUSAND CASTS

some dinner right now . . . looks like this here storms gonna last awhile so ya might as well make yerselfs at home."

"We'd love to!" Wally and I answered.

"What!?" Beef exclaimed. "Are you guys crazy? Lets just get the inner tubes and get the . . ."

Beef stopped in mid sentence for from outside emerged a petite young woman with long blonde hair. Her rain drenched sun dress clung to her body revealing several voluptuous curves. I guessed her age at 20 or 21 and even Wally and I were temporarily paralyzed by her natural beauty. Darn! Maybe it wasn't wise for me to admit to being married after all. Beef, a notorious woman chaser, was immediately smitten.

"Dinner sounds nice," Beef continued. "I don't know why you guys are in such a hurry, it's raining like hell out there!"

"Hi! I'm Fannie Sue," the young woman said to Beef. "Is this one fer me Paw?"

"He shore is honey bunch! Didn't I tells ya I'd find ya a man?" Paw answered.

Beef was too entranced with Fannie's curves to notice the conversation around him and she was equally smitten with Beef.

"Yer kinda cute," she said. "Ya wanna see ma kitty?"

Beef's eyes popped open so much that I thought they were going to explode out of his head. He nodded weakly and followed Fannie Sue into the living room.

The kitty in question was named Morris. Morris was not an actual household cat but rather a large bobcat. He was curled up in an ancient looking chair and snarled at the sight of three strangers walking into his territory. His head was as big as a basketball and he would rival a German Shepherd in the size department. Morris was, indeed, a fitting member of this odd family.

Also in the living room were two other individuals. A young woman who appeared to be in her mid twenties was sitting in a chair knitting. Her name was Eva and she was, quite obviously, with child. The knitting, no doubt, was for her expected arrival. Sitting beside her, on the floor, was a scrawny young man with a face that seemed familiar to me. I studied the face, as I knew I had seen this person before.

"Stinky, don't be so rude," said the pregnant woman. "Get up and introduce yerself to the nice men!"

Stinky? Why of course! It was hard to recognize him with his facial stubble, but the young man was Stinky Peterson, a kid that we knew from high school. Stinky's claim to fame was an inadvertent act of flatulence that occurred during the silence of study hall. He never lived that event down during high school and after graduation he disappeared into nothingness... never to be seen again.

"Uh... Hi," Stinky said.

Dean finally emerged from the upstairs followed by The Squirrel who was decked out in his "new" set of clothes. Picture if you can the spectacle of the Squirrel's attire. He was wearing a pair of Dean's bib overalls and they were, at least, six sizes too big. The Squirrel is 5'4" tall and weighs 130lbs on a good day. Dean was well over 6 feet tall and probably tipped the scales at 300—easy. One lone strap across the shoulders held the massive bibs to The Squirrels narrow frame and the ensemble was completed with an oversized pair of work boots! All that was missing was a straw hat and corncob pipe. Wally and I had a hard time concealing our laughter.

"Shut up guys! This is not the least bit amusing," The Squirrel said. The pitch of his voice was rising, as it's prone to do when he becomes agitated.

"Well, I kinda like the duds on you boy," said Paw. "Yer fittin' into the family already."

Maw came out of the kitchen to meet the newest stranger.

"This here the fella you got picked out for Eula?" asked Maw.

THE FISH OF A THOUSAND CASTS

"Yep . . . he needs a little fattening up but I think he'll do jist fine," Paw answered.

"Well, he is a might scrawny," Maw commented as she poked at The Squirrel with a wooden spoon. "But my cookin' will put some meat on his bones. Dean! Tell Eula to git down here an meet this fella."

"Eula? Who's Eula?" asked The Squirrel.

"Eula's my twin sister!" answered Fannie Sue.

The Squirrels face erupted in a giant grin. He, just like Beef, is a seasoned girl chaser.

Suddenly, the house began to shake. We thought it was from the storm at first but the shaking became much more intense. It was footsteps! Someone was coming down from upstairs and each step grew louder and louder and louder until . . . *she* came through the door.

"*You call that a twin?*" The Squirrel shrieked as his jaw dropped to the floor.

Eula. Big Eula. Huge Eula. As long as I live, I will never forget Eula. She was close to seven feet tall and the only similarity between her and Fannie Sue was the color of their hair. Where Fannie was petite, Eula was, shall we say, *not*. Her greasy blonde hair was in pigtails and she wore a cut off T-shirt and Daisy Duke shorts that did nothing except make the numerous fat rolls more pronounced. If anything, she was more like Dean's twin! She looked down at The Squirrel and clapped her mighty hands together.

"Oh paw!" Eula squealed. "Is this here man fer me? Oh he's so cute . . . he looks like a little squirrel!"

Eula scooped our poor comrade into her arms and wrapped him in a giant bear hug. The Squirrel tried to slither free of her "loving" embrace but to no avail. Eula wasn't about to give up her prized possession.

"Isn't that cute?" said Maw. "Well . . . I got to git back to fixin' dinner. Girls, git in this kitchen an make yerselves useful. Show yer new men how you can cook!"

Fannie Sue planted a little kiss on Beefs cheek, Eula smiled at The Squirrel revealing a missing front tooth and both exited toward the kitchen.

"That's it!" The Squirrel snapped. "I'm outta here!"

"Hang on dude," Beef said. "I think I can get lucky!"

"You think you can get *what* boy?" Paw snarled. "There ain't goin' ta be no ruttin' goin' on in this house until *after* the weddin'."

"Weddin'*? What weddin'*?" Beef gulped.

Things were starting to get tense so Wally, ever the diplomat, tried to change the subject.

"I see you have a lot of antiques here. I'm quite an antique buff myself," he said. "Why, I'll bet that TV there is almost fifty years old . . . how about that?"

"Yep it shore is," Paw answered, settling down. "But we ain't had much use fer it since they stopped showin' Hee Haw."

As Paw said that, everyone in the house lowered their heads and became silent. Obviously, the loss of their beloved Hee-Haw still affected them to that very day. It was kind of sad.

The storm continued to rage as the pleasant aroma of home cooking filled the house. To pass the time, Paw put on his favorite record album, "Roy Clarks Greatest Hits", and told us about the kind of simple life that his family lead. Deep down inside, you could sense that he was a good man, dedicated to protecting his family.

Finally, dinner was laid out on the table and it was quite a spread I can assure you. We had fried chicken, mashed potatoes, corn, and asparagus. These simple folk sure knew how to eat! We ate that magnificent dinner and Paw continued telling Wally and I about his way of life.

"Ya see boys, this here valley used ta belong to the simple folk like us. As time went by, we was the only ones left. Every one else up and moved to the city but . . . I cain't do that. My

THE FISH OF A THOUSAND CASTS

heart is right here on ma land. Trouble is, back in the old days, a father didn't have ta worry bout his daughters growin' up lonely ol' maids. There was always some fine young men who would come around courtin' and treat em wit respect. Now all's they think about is ruttin'. Shoot, they don't even think they got's ta show respect fer the Paw no more."

"Well, I certainly think that you deserve that respect sir," Wally said. "You seem like a nice guy to me."

"Hang on a sec... Maw! Put some more food on that there boys plate," Paw ordered, referring to The Squirrel. "I cain't have ma son in law lookin' so scrawny!"

"So... son... son in... what? *EXCUSE ME?*" The Squirrel shrieked. He was doing a lot of shrieking lately.

"Yer right boys. I am a nice guy but there comes a time when I got's to protect ma daughters. That's why, come tomorrow, them two boys there is gonna get hitched to my little girls!"

Wally and I gagged on our food, Eula squealed with delight, and The Squirrel passed out cold, his face landing in a pile of mashed potatoes. Beef was too busy making goo goo eyes at Fannie Sue to hear any of the conversation and just nodded his head in agreement.

"Uh huh... this chicken is good," he mumbled.

After dinner, we were ordered into the living room for "quality time" as Paw called it. Up on the mantle of the fireplace was an ancient radio. Paw was a big baseball fan and the Detroit Tigers were playing that night. The entire family stared at the radio as the voice of Ernie Harwell reverberated throughout the room and described every nuance of the ball game. It was dark out now and the storm wasn't letting up. The Squirrel was still unconscious and Eula was applying a cold rag to his forehead. Every time he started to come to, he'd take one look at Eula's face and out he would go again. Wally and I were enjoying a huge helping of homemade cherry cobbler for desert. It was absolutely delicious. Beef and Fannie Sue were noticeably absent from the proceedings. Somehow, they'd managed to slip out of the room undetected.

"If I don't get back home soon, my wife is going to kill me," I whispered to Wally.

"I know... mine too," he whispered back.

With that, we looked at each other and it was understood. Beef and The Squirrel were on their own. First chance we could get, Wally and I were getting out of there!

All we needed was a distraction and thankfully our prayers were about to be answered.

"Eula, where'd yor sista go?" Paw asked, raising his eyebrow at Wally and I.

"I dunno Paw... her and her fella left a little while ago."

Paw jumped up from his chair and started down the hallway. Wally and I braced ourselves for a quick exit and The Squirrel moaned weakly. Paw stopped in front of a door, pressed his ear against it and then kicked it open.

"What in tarnation!" he bellowed. "Boy, you actin' like you *already* married!"

"What do you mean... *already?*" Beef said.

"Dean! Bring me ma razor strap!" Paw continued screaming. "You gonna have respect fer yer Paw in law boy!"

"Don't hurt em Paw! Don't hurt em Paw!" Fannie pleaded. "We wasn't doin' no ruttin' yet!"

"*Yet?* Dean! Git in here with ma strap!"

Maw gasped something about "Good Lord Jesus" before *she* passed out cold and Stinky and Eva rushed to her aid while everything unfolded. Paw shouted, Beef argued, and Dean grabbed the razor strap.

"Kill, kill, kill, kill, kill!" he grunted as he plodded down the hall.

The shouting continued and the crack of the razor strap was heard. Dean bellowed out in agony because the first strike of the strap hit him instead of Beef. Fannie kept pleading Beef's case and the ruckus spilled into the hallway.

THE FISH OF A THOUSAND CASTS

With cat like reflexes, Beef dove under Paws legs and started running down the hall. Paw and Dean were close on his tail as Beef crashed into the living room and Eula jumped up to stop him. As soon as Eula got up, The Squirrel regained consciousness, saw his chance for escape, and quickly shot out the front door. Beef hurtled the couch, dodged another swipe from the razor strap and scurried out the front door.

"Wee Haw!" shouted Paw. "We got us a couple a run aways!"

"Let's get em Paw!" Dean said as they gave chase; Eula and Fannie Sue joined in.

Wally and I finished the last of our cherry cobbler and sat the empty plates on the coffee table next to the couch.

"Shall we?" I said to Wally.

"Yep, I believe it's time to go," he answered, wiping cherry juice off his chin.

We both stood up and started walking, nonchalantly, toward the back porch. Most of the commotion outside was taking place in the front of the house. We were about to walk through the back door when we felt a hand grab our shoulders.

"You boys goin' somewhere?"

It was Stinky! In all the madness, we completely forgot about him being there! Damn ... we were busted.

"If your gonna make it down the trail, your gonna need this," he said.

He handed us a flashlight, patted us on the back and wished us good luck. He let us go! Stinky wasn't a member of the family after all and it became quite clear that his marriage to Eva was "arranged" by Paw. How else could you explain him helping us out like that?

Wally and I stepped on to the back porch and there, in front of us, laid Morris. Morris took one look at us and decided that fresh meat was better than the chicken bone he was gnawing on. He slowly stood up and snarled.

"Heh heh, nice Kitty," Wally said.

The Squirrel dashed into the backyard with Dean right behind. Morris jumped off the porch and started chasing The Squirrel.

"Kill, Morris! Kill Kill!" Dean hollered.

Morris got right behind The Squirrel and vaulted into the air . . .

RRRRRRRRRRRRRRIP!!!!!!

Morris had grabbed ahold of the oversized bibs and they tore off, saving The Squirrel from a good maiming. The large bobcat growled and snarled as he wrestled with the pile of empty clothes. Much to our disgust, The Squirrel was darting around the yard buck naked, except for the pair of mammoth sized work boots that he still had on! Maw had regained her senses and was bound and determined to find a switch.

"Trying to violate my baby girl under my own roof?" she muttered to herself as she broke off a suitable "whipping" branch from a weeping willow tree in the front yard. "I'll tan that hide until he cain't sit down!"

Wally and I sauntered to the end of the back yard, clicked on the flash light and made our way down the trail to our inner tubes. In the distance, we could still hear the sounds of Beef and The Squirrel engaged in their escape.

"Boy, put yer clothes back on and show some respect fer ma little girls!" we heard Paw screaming.

"Bring me back ma little squirrel, Paw!" Eula sobbed.

"When I gits ma hands on you two yer gonna learn respect fer yore Paw in Law!"

The shouting and screaming grew more faint as we drifted down stream. The clouds were clearing and a few stars were shining in the night sky. Finally, it was peaceful and the only sounds to be heard were the frogs and the bubbling of the river.

"Ya know, Wally," I said, staring up at the newly emerged stars. "Maybe I'm just getting a bit older, but these little trips of ours just don't seem to have the excitement that they used to."

"Yeah," he sighed, "I know what you mean . . . nothing out of the ordinary seems to happen anymore."

We heard the sound of Beef and the naked Squirrel dive into the river just behind us.

"I feel bad for The Squirrel," I said, "this water's pretty cold."

"At least Beef has his swim trunks on!"

The Canoe Race

The arrival of spring is greeted in many ways. Most of the time, it involves an event, festival, or other jovial gathering. People in Omer celebrate the onset of spring with their famous "Sucker Fest". Benton Harbor has its Blossom Parade and various other communities have their flea markets and carnivals. I, like many people, feel a rebirth of sorts when the days grow longer. A simple walk through the woods in search of Morels is a welcome relief from the blustery effects of a prolonged Michigan winter.

Growing up in my beloved Hillsdale County, there was always one event that for me signaled the arrival of spring, the annual canoe race.

We don't have a great deal of excitement in Hillsdale County and the canoe race qualified as a full-blown event in our little section of the state. People actually travel from all parts of the state to participate in this competition and it even gets broadcast on the local radio station!

It begins at one end of Baw Beese Lake, which is located in Hillsdale, continues into the St. Joseph River, and finally ends six miles downstream in the town of Jonesville. "Mill Race Days", a festival in Jonesville, coincides with the canoe race. The race itself, is an exercise in discipline, physical stress, and mental toughness. Navigating six miles of river requires good physical training and many professional canoeists participate; most of the people who compete, however, could hardly be considered "good physical specimens". The allure of the race is to witness who collapses from exhaustion first. Of the locals that entered, most never trained a lick for the big race. In fact, half of them didn't even own a canoe!

My father, The Chief, once lent his canoe to a couple of his buddies for the race. The Chief takes great pride in his canoes and he was a little displeased when the canoe was returned beat up and dented. Once the canoeists enter the St. Joe, it becomes a demolition derby as well as a race. The river isn't very wide in this part of the state and passing other canoes requires a little smashing and crashing. Throw in the assorted rocks, logs, and numerous portages and things tend to get a little messy. The current in the river isn't swift enough to coast along so you really have to keep paddling if you want to make good time. Consider all that and it's really a great deal of fun just being a spectator.

One spring, Beef and The Squirrel grew tired of being spectators and they decided to sign up for the race. Neither one of them had a canoe so they approached me about a possible loaner. My canoe had seen better days so it was no problem for me to loan it to them. Hell, I'd have loaned them a brand new canoe if it meant watching them embarrass themselves! I know my limitations and I wasn't about to attempt the rigors of the race. Those two failed to recognize their lack of physical health and thus provided me with enough material to base this story around. Beef and The Squirrel in a canoe race? What more could I ask for!

At that point in my life, I was experimenting with outdoor writing and as a result I decided to keep a diary of sorts on their racing experience. One of my favorite McManus stories is done in diary form so I made a poor attempt to emulate that style of writing. If anything, I figured it would be kind of neat to look back on when we were older. How I hung on to it this long is beyond me.

9:50 AM:

Beef and The Squirrel are preparing for the race. My canoe is number 42 and is in the first row of canoes to be launched. The start of the race is at famous Sandy Beach. Beef and The Squirrel will have to canoe the entire length of the lake (about one mile) before they even get to the entrance of the St. Joe River. Beef and The Squirrel psyched themselves up for the race by attending a "gathering" the night before that lasted until 5:00am. Neither appears to have recovered from the effects of this "gathering" and I anticipate their participation in this event to be short and sweet.

10:00 AM:

The race is underway. Race participants are launched in heats of 10 canoes. Every 5 minutes, a new heat is launched. Beef and The Squirrel are in the first heat and have vaulted out to an early lead. Unbelievable!

10:01 AM:

The initial rush of adrenaline has finally worn off and the rest of the pack has caught up with them. Look at the bright side though, at least they led the race for *15 yards*! That's more than could be expected of those two.

THE FISH OF A THOUSAND CASTS

10:02 AM:

Beef and The Squirrel have settled into a deliberate but steady pace. I will drive down to the other end of the lake and wait for them to enter the St. Joe River...

10:30 AM:

Racers from the first four heats have entered the river and yet Beef and the Squirrel are no where to be found. Several of the race participants were commenting about a scrawny individual who "tossed his cookies" numerous times. Based on their descriptions, I can only conclude that the vomiting individual is The Squirrel. They're getting ready to launch the "Under 14 year old" division of racers at 10:45 am.

I can see my canoe now; Beef and The Squirrel are trailing the fifth and final heat.

10:35 AM:

They've finally entered the river. The Squirrel, looking quite pale, complained of extreme fatigue and asked me to kindly "kill" him. Beef was disgusted at The Squirrel's lack of vomit control and had his feet propped up on the center support to avoid making contact with The Squirrels breakfast; which was presently meandering around the bottom of the canoe. I'll be waiting for them at the first portage downstream.

10:47 AM:

The first portage is complete. The Squirrel looks to have gained a second wind and things appear to be looking up as they are now comfortably in last place. Beef took the opportunity during the portage to quickly wash the foul remains of breakfast from the bottom of the canoe. Both canoe and Squirrel appear to be in good health. Next portage: Stocks Park, downstream.

11:01 AM:

My canoe and its passengers are approaching the next portage at Stocks Park. This is a fairly difficult portage because it involves carrying a canoe across the bridge and down stream beyond the expanse of chain link fence that surrounds the local flourmill. Total distance to carry canoe: 75 yards. The previous racers picked up their canoes and sprinted the entire distance. They've obviously trained well for this event. The bridge in question is too low to the water to travel under thus necessitating the need to portage.

Beef and The Squirrel have decided to take their chances with going under the bridge in an attempt to pick up time. Both are currently crouched in the bottom of the canoe and will use what little current there is to push them along.

The Squirrel gives me a thumbs up and says, "Don't worry! We'll make it!" as the canoe disappears under the bridge.

12:17 PM:

The canoe and its occupants have finally been dislodged from under the bridge! It was quite an ordeal due to The Squirrels case of claustrophobia. His muffled high-pitched screams echoed from under the confines of the bridge causing several locals to take notice. The radio station caught wind of the trapped racers and kept giving live updates on the progress of their rescue. The efforts of the local rescue squad were to no avail, as they didn't have the type of equipment needed for dislodging a canoe from under a bridge. As The Squirrel's panic attacks led him to hyperventilation, I decided to take drastic measures to assist my comrades. I paid one of the

THE FISH OF A THOUSAND CASTS

local children, a 10-year old boy named Edgar, to crawl under the bridge and tie a rope to the front of the canoe. Several of us were able to pull the canoe out from under the bridge and into the God saving embrace of fresh air.

The Squirrel and Beef are, at this point, way behind every canoe in the race. The entire "Under 14" division is now well downstream. The two morons have vowed to keep going despite the fact that they're on course to set a new, all county, record for canoe race futility.

I made mental note to remind Beef and The Squirrel to reimburse me the $5.00 it cost for their rescue.

It will be awhile before I report again as the next viewing spot is at Mauck Road, two and a half miles down river. The rigor of documenting the moron's journey has made me hungry. I'm joining The Chief at The Queasy Kitchen and will not report again until *after* lunch.

2:45 PM:

Well, the canoe race is over. Every single canoe, except for one, has crossed the finish line. The lone exception, which is passengered by The Squirrel and Beef, has yet to make it to Mauck Road. The Chief and I have been waiting here for 20 minutes. The Chief is currently napping at the side of the riverbank and I'm listening to the Red Wings game on the radio.

The topic of the afternoon at the diner was, of course, the two individuals who were trapped under the bridge. Several suggestions were made as to their rationale in attempting such a "fool thing" and most blamed it on alcohol consumption. Someone recognized me and asked if I was friends with the two drunkards. I denied any knowledge of their existence and continued to dine on my hamburger.

The Red Wings are well in control of the hockey game so I myself am inclined to take a short nap . . .

3:28 PM:

The sound of a canoe paddle banging against a canoe has stirred me from my nap. The two morons have finally reached the Mauck Road Bridge. As they passed under it, I noticed that both of them were sporting a number of bright red welts. From what I can gather, Beef and The Squirrel were passing under a tree that contained a large hornet's nest. In one of those rare instances where point A intersects with point B and all of the planets in the Milky Way align properly, the branch that was holding the nest gave way just as the canoe was passing under it. Much to the surprise of the morons, the nest landed right in the middle of the canoe. The residents of the nest were none too pleased about their relocation and decided to take their anger out on the first things they saw. Beef and The Squirrel tried to take cover in the water, but since the water in question was only six inches deep, their efforts to seek refuge were futile.

Perhaps it was a sign from above, an attempt to convince them to call it a day. The two heathens have chosen to ignore the divine intervention and finish the race.

The next viewing area is the Jonesville millpond. A fine golf course borders the entire length of the millpond so The Chief and I have decided to play a round of nine and monitor the moron's progress from the fairway.

5:15 PM:

The Chief and I are almost through with our golf game. The hole we're playing sits atop a hill that overlooks the millpond. The canoe containing Beef and The Squirrel is going along at a pretty good pace. An amazing feat considering that The Squirrel is slumped over the front of the canoe, motionless, and Beef is paddling by himself. The reason that Beef is paddling with such vigor is due to a pair of red wing blackbirds that seem to be buzzing the canoe. It looks as if the canoe passed too close to a nesting area and red wing blackbirds are extremely ferocious when protecting their young.

Beef is now standing up in the canoe and swinging his paddle at the birds. Bad things happen when you stand up in a canoe. It's my turn to putt, be back in a minute...

5:18 PM:

Not bad, I birdied the hole! Speaking of birdies, the pair of black birds have ended their assault and returned to the nest. Beef and The Squirrel have swum to shore with the canoe in tow and are now portaging over the Jonesville Dam. I can't hear what's being said but it looks as if The Squirrel is upset with Beef for standing up in the canoe and thus tipping it over. Keep your heads together guys! Only one more mile to go. The fact that they actually portaged the dam instead of going over it proves that they're starting to get the hang of this canoe stuff.

At the pace they're going, The Chief and I will have plenty of time to finish our game and have dinner before Moron Inc. crosses the finish line.

7:30 PM:

The moronic duo hasn't arrived yet. Most of the people attending "Mill Race Days" have vacated the finish area and our now assembled at the popular "Hillsdale Gun and Muffin Club Beer Tent". The Chief grew tired of waiting for the last place racers and decided to join the town folk in the beer tent. I, the loyal friend, have decided to ignore the festivities in the tent and wait for my two companions.

7:41 PM:

Beef and The Squirrel are now in sight of the finish line! Closer... closer... closer... they did it! They actually completed the race. The Squirrel has decided to celebrate by passing out near the riverbank. Beef is still sitting in the canoe and refuses to get out. He's mumbling something about his body being too stiff to move and is now requesting assistance. I'll have to wrap this thing up now and help my two idiot friends. In conclusion, they have set a new record time for completing the canoe race, nine hours and forty one minutes, the worst time in the history of the race.

Congratulations Gentlemen!

Snow, Steelies and The Big "V"

Beef and I paid a visit to our good friend Wally. His wife nervously paced the house, as she doesn't like Beef or myself, but didn't say much because she knew we were on a mission of mercy.

"How ya feelin' old buddy?" I asked. Wally was sprawled out on the couch with an ice bag covering his ... well ... sensitive area.

"I'm a little sore," he answered. "Feels like I got kicked!"

"I'd be more than sore if they cut mine off!" Beef pointed out.

"They don't cut 'em off," Wally answered. "What do you guys want?"

Before I continue, allow me to explain that Wally's predicament was self-induced. You see he and his wife felt that with three children they'd contributed enough to society. Since there was now plenty of offspring to carry on the family name, Wally was elected to undergo *"The Big V"*. I think you know what I'm talking about. I'd recently gone through the Big D, but at least that painless, and welcome, extraction didn't involve surgery. Wally was now recovering and Beef and I felt his recovery would be faster if he got out and enjoyed some fine winter steelheading. The cold Michigan air would do him some good . . . maybe reduce the swelling, who knows?

"What do we want? What kind of question is that?" I said. "Get your coat, we're hitting the river!"

"Hitting the river? I'm in pain!" Wally shot back. "I'm not leaving this couch for anything!"

"I can't blame you," Beef spoke up. "I wouldn't want to do nothin' but lay around either if I got mine cut off . . ."

"They don't cut 'em off," I said to Beef. "Now quit whining, Wallace, and get your rod and waders . . . we're angels on a mission of mercy here."

"Angels? You two?" Wally's wife snorted. "More like the angels of death . . ."

As I said before, Wally's wife doesn't like us, but that was neither here nor there at the moment. Undaunted by her snide remark, we continued on in our mission of mercy. Wally was adamant about not joining us for a little fishing. He was bound and determined to stay on that couch. He argued and refused even as he sprawled himself out in the back of my Explorer.

"You'll feel a lot better," I said as we backed out of his driveway. "A little fishing will take your mind off the pain."

"How would you two know about the pain?" he whined. "It's not like you've been through this! So you forced me off my couch, that doesn't mean that I'm going to get out of this backseat . . ."

"You know," Beef said. "I remember this old dog my grandparents had. He kept running around every night and the neighborhood was over run with puppies. They finally took him to the vet and that poor dog didn't want to do anything afterwards. It was like they removed his soul. I felt bad for him you know?"

"And your point would be?" Wally asked.

"Oh, no point," Beef answered. "I just feel sorry for you that's all. I know I could never get mine cut off that's for sure..."

"They don't cut them off!" Wally and I shouted in unison.

A heavy snow was falling as we made our way to the Dowagiac River in Niles, a favorite destination of ours for winter Steelhead. The Dowagiac has a large mixture of summer run fish and fall fish so we usually had pretty good luck there. When we arrived I had two choices, I could park at the easy access parking lot or I could slap the Explorer in four wheel drive and navigate a rough two track back to some isolated holes.

Wally began whining as the vehicle bounced along the two track.

"Ouch!" he shouted. "Is there a particular reason you're doing this? EEK! Why didn't you just park back in the lot? OOF!"

"Just hang on to your ice bag," I countered. "We'll be there in a minute."

When I finally stopped the vehicle, Wally was glaring at me as a cold sweat ran down his face. I could tell that he wanted to unleash a flood of vulgarities but that's not his nature. He did everything to restrain himself. The snow continued to fall at a blinding pace...

"Ah... doesn't get much better than this," I said. "There's nothing like being on the river in the middle of a snowstorm."

"Yeah... let me know how it is," Wally said. "I'm just gonna lay here with my ice bag and wait for you guys..."

There is an overpowering urge to winter steelheading that cannot be ignored. Wally tried to ignore it but as Beef and I donned our waders and began rigging our rods, he started to flash a little enthusiasm and finally relented to our mission of mercy.

"You know... maybe I'll make a few casts after all." Wally said.

Our trek to the water was delayed a bit as Wally slowly snugged his waders up to his chest, wincing all the while. He positioned the ice bag inside his waders for maximum relief and hobbled along the narrow trail down to the water's edge.

The spot we chose to fish was a long, deep hole that ran the entire length of a wide river bend. Winter steelies often like to hold in such areas and we'd had decent luck there in the past. At the tailout of the bend were several logjams that made fighting a fish tricky if you let them run that far. A layer of shelf ice created a small ledge at the riverbank.

"Anybody got a bobber?" Wally asked. "I left mine up in the truck."

"If you were in good health, I'd make you walk back up there and get them," I said, "but since I'm feeling benevolent today, I'll let you use one of mine..."

"I'd make him walk," Beef stated. "He did this to himself..."

When it comes to fishing for Steelhead in the dead of winter, bobbers are like gold. We die hard anglers horde them like kids with a stash of Halloween candy. It was a great sacrifice for me to give one up to Wally thus proving that I was, indeed, on a mission of mercy. Under different circumstances, I'd have made him walk.

Now, despite the fact that when the three of us get together certain bad things happen, I will say that we do pretty well when it comes to hooking fish. A spawn bag under a bobber is our standard offering of choice and we take a lot of fish with that, but when things are slow we break out the "secret weapon". The secret weapon is nothing more than a wax worm. Put a wax worm under a bobber and you'll get fish. It's as simple as that. The bobber is the key, however,

THE FISH OF A THOUSAND CASTS

and the reason we value them so much. Winter steelies are a pretty lazy bunch and the only sure-fire way to tell if they hit is to watch your bobber go down. I've tried doing it by feel but with cold, numb fingers, you don't feel much. Heck, I've had steelies inhale the wax worm, chew on it for awhile like bubble gum, swish it around their mouth a few times and then spit it out. All the while my numb fingers never felt a thing. With a bobber, you can at least wear gloves!

The three of us lined up on the ice ledge and began casting into the hole. The snow at this point was coming down so hard that we had it piling up on the top of our heads and we could barely see our bobbers.

"You know, this is pretty peaceful just standing here," Wally said. "I really don't feel that uncomfortable!"

"See? I told you so . . . beats laying around on the couch feeling sorry for yourself." I answered.

We kept casting and finally my bobber went down. A nice buck steelie, maybe 6 pounds or so, decided my pink spawn bag would make a good snack. He was pretty lethargic and after a quick battle, I removed the hook and allowed the vanquished creature to wander back to the depths of his hole to sulk for awhile. It wasn't long after that when Wally's bobber went under. He set the hook and realized he was into a fish much bigger than mine.

"Whoa! I think this ones a biggie!" he grunted.

The fish darted back and forth around the pool as Wally kept pressure on the rod. In an instance, the fish leaped from the water in spectacular fashion revealing his enormous length and girth.

Everything goes in slow motion when you're out on the river. What happens in a second seems like minutes. The fish was in full winter colors and as he hung in midair you could almost count his spots. He had a brilliant crimson streak down his side and a gnarly hooked jaw that showed he was a pretty nefarious figure in the underwater crime syndicate. Other fish most certainly avoided this character, as he was probably the type of bully that would push you down and steal your milk money! He hit the water with a resounding and magnificent splash. Soon after, he made a break for one of the logjams.

"You better follow him or else he's going to get in those logs!" Beef pointed out.

Wally shuffled along the slippery ice ledge as best he could. The faster he moved, the more he started to grimace. He was obviously in a great deal of discomfort and most of us would have said, "Nope... I'm not risking further pain by chasing a stupid fish," but this was the biggest steelie of Wally's life and he wasn't about to let a few ripped stitches deter him from subduing this thug.

Despite his efforts, the beast went under one of the logs, turned around and headed back upstream. Wally's line was wrapped around the log as his bobber went scooting by him in the opposite direction.

"Hey... he's still on," Wally said, "what should I do?"

"See if you can get your line out from under the log!" I answered. "Go out a little further on that ice ledge and see if you can run your rod tip under the log..."

"I don't know how safe that ice is!" he shouted back.

"Just put one foot on the log and the other on the ice... it will take some weight off the ledge," I said. "What's the worst that could happen?"

Wally did as instructed. He put one foot on the log, left the other on the ledge and was beginning to get his fishing line out from under the log when... the worst thing happened.

It was so slow, that it is painful just to describe it. First, there was a loud cracking sound and Wally's eyes shifted downward with a look of panic. Immediately thereafter, a section of the ice ledge broke free and began drifting away. Apparently, the excessive snow and cold caused the felt on the bottom of Wally's wader boot to adhere to the ice. As the

THE FISH OF A THOUSAND CASTS

ledge drifted away, Wally's legs began getting further and further apart. He began to scream. It wasn't a normal scream, mind you, but more like a high pitched wail. Beef and I were helpless and could only wince as Wally sunk lower and lower; his legs separating all the while. It was painfully slow. Wally reminded us of his faith in the Lord by summoning up numerous "Good Lord help me!" and "Sweet Jesus have mercy!" phrases mixed in with his high pitched wails. I was amazed at the absence of profanity in all of this. Weaker individuals, like myself, would've used up every vernacular in existence and even created a few new ones! But that's Wally, God fearing and focused . . . even under the direst of circumstances. The agonizing descent continued and when it was all said and done Wally had performed the splits so well that a teenaged cheerleader would have stood in envy and asked for pointers. His legs were completely straight out in opposite directions.

"Did you get the line out from under there?" Beef finally asked.

Wally's response cannot be printed here but, suffice to say, he was going to have to go to confession when he got home. Even I was shocked that such vulgarity could escape the lips of a God fearing man like Wally. Everyone has their breaking point.

As Wally hung inches above the water with legs spread wide, the fish grew tired due to the pressure on the line and began thrashing on the surface. I waded out to him and slipped the net under it. He was a pig . . . almost twenty pounds! Beef got Wally dislodged from the ledge and helped him back to shore.

It was the biggest steelie of his life and Wally decided to have it mounted. All the way back home, Wally didn't say a word. He simply lay in the back of the Explorer; cradling the fish and whimpering like a lost puppy. We helped him back to his couch where he didn't move for almost three days. His doctor figured that Wally had set his recovery back by more than a week.

"Why is he blaming us?" Beef asked. "He shouldn't have been out if he just got 'em cut off!"

"I know!" I said. "The doctor told him to just take it easy and relax."

"Some people just never take responsibility for their own actions!"

White Tailed Annie's New Tattoo

I made a cast into the rust colored, slow current of the Au Sable River. The large bell sinker made a loud "plop" as it entered the water, sending another plump night crawler to it's doom. After placing the rod into the makeshift rod holder, I flopped back into my lawn chair and gazed up at all the shining stars. It was a beautiful summer night.

Beef and I were a bit unsettled, of course. Beautiful nights are not the norm when we take to the water. We kept looking up at the stars. Where were the storm clouds? Where was the wind? We kept waiting for a storm front or a fog bank . . . anything. The madness was almost unbearable!

We were on our annual "Sheephead" expedition in Oscoda, Michigan. It started out years ago as a catfish expedition after we'd read an article in Woods N Water News about the fantastic channel cat fishery at the mouth of the Au Sable. The author was holding up a giant, gray, catfish and we decided to give it a try. All we caught was a bunch of grunting sheephead, but had a blast in the process. It is now a much-anticipated portion of our yearly schedule of events and almost rivals our annual salmon vacation.

Wally and The Squirrel were with us, but they'd ventured into town to grab a bite to eat. Their lawn chairs and fishing poles were sitting on the cement boardwalk that leads to the long pier into the harbor.

The trip started out promising. As we headed north up I-75, the sky was black and churning. Beef, The Squirrel, and I came up earlier in the afternoon. Getting a later start, Wally had to negotiate with his significant other and was granted permission to attend the trip on the condition that he'd refrain from any activities that I suggested. Apparently, his young son had learned some choice words and strangely enough, he learned them right after a trip onto Lake Michigan with Wally and myself. For a week or so, after the trip, Wally Jr. would playfully mention the words in all kinds of settings: Church, Daycare, Grandma's house, etc. Wally's wife reasoned that her fine, upstanding, husband would never utter such words and by process of elimination, I was targeted as the bad influence. She's always viewed me as a bad influence and the "words incident" only added fuel to the fire, hence her reluctance in letting Wally attend this years trip.

As I was saying, the sky was churning black as the three of us traveled up the highway. My Explorer rattled and shook as rain and hail splattered all around. Lightening bolts danced across the sky and the wind was roaring. Nothing out of the ordinary there. Beef and I yawned when a tornado cut across the highway, picking up a motor home from a storage place and dropping it right in our path. I swerved around that, dodged an uprooted oak tree, and continued north toward our destination. Mother Nature, quite frustrated that her little onslaught had failed to bother us, quickly relented and the sky was blue once again.

THE FISH OF A THOUSAND CASTS

"Did I miss anything?" The Squirrel asked as he awoke from a short nap.

"Nothing out of the ordinary," Beef answered.

Ordinary was the key word on this trip. Beef and I stared at our rod tips, waiting for a hit. The fishing was quite good, but the evident lack of surprise was gnawing at us. Beef had just changed into dry clothes after his little tumble off the pier. He bounced off some large boulders before hitting the water and had a noticeable limp afterwards. Wally managed to lose a rod when a large carp picked up his night crawler and headed toward the lake. The rod flew out of the rod holder and entered the water like a javelin. Somehow, my hook caught the rod as it scraped across the bottom and we were able to retrieve the rod as well as the thieving carp. The Squirrel and I thought it would be cute to feed the seagulls, but there were more of them than we thought. Soon, a massive flock ambushed us and while fleeing the pecking creatures we were forced to take refuge under the Explorer until the angry mob subsided. This trip was getting quite boring since nothing out of the ordinary was happening!

Boredom hovered over us and the tedium was unbearable. Something had to happen, anything. This was, shudder the thought, getting peaceful and relaxing. We were listening to a Tigers game on the radio and I was thinking about taking a little nap when I caught a glimpse of someone staggering down the pier in our direction. As the figure got closer, I could see that it was a fairly petite and attractive female, maybe 25 years old, give or take a little. She was quite intoxicated it appeared. She clutched a bottle of cheap wine in one hand and braced herself on the railing with the other.

"Hey Beef," I said, "check this out!"

"Way ahead of you!" he answered.

The young lady wearing a small T-shirt and sweat pants, reached the end of the pier, stumbled down the short metal steps, somersaulted across the concrete boardwalk and landed with a loud thump right at my feet.

"Hello," she said without missing a beat. "My name's Annie!"

"Well hello, Annie," I answered, looking down at her sprawled out on the concrete. "Nasty little spill you took there. Are you alright?"

"Couldn' be better," she slurred. "I didn' even shpill my wine!"

Annie sat back up and what followed was the most annoying torture I've ever been subjected to! Annie began to babble endlessly about nothing in particular. She heard the game on our radio and babbled about how much she loved the Tigers. Then she rambled about her favorite wine, followed by her choice of magazines. In between large gulps of wine, she explained that her boyfriend, a "six foot six, full blooded Huron Indian, named Ripper" was fishing at the end of the pier. He'd taken up fishing as a form of anger management and wasn't paying any attention to her, so she decided to go for a little walk. Babble, babble, babble . . .

I wasn't about to suffer alone, so I invited Beef into the "conversation".

"This is my good friend Beef," I introduced. "Beef, this is Annie."

Annie stood up and extended her hand toward Beef. In the process, she tripped over the radio and landed face down on the concrete. Beef and I jumped up from our lawn chairs and helped her to her feet.

"Whew," Annie sighed, "almost shpilled it that time!"

I tried to sneak back to my lawn chair. Beef looked to the heavens and whispered, "Thank you, God" while Annie started her drunken babbling again. After she'd exhausted any and all topics of conversation she mentioned something about her "new tattoo", that peaked our interest.

"You got a tattoo, huh?" Beef asked. "Let's see it!"

THE FISH OF A THOUSAND CASTS

"You wanna shee it? Really?" Annie questioned.

"Sure," Beef answered. "Let's have a look!"

Annie took a big swig of her wine. We expected her to roll up her shirtsleeve and reveal the tattoo. Instead, Annie spun around, bent over and dropped her sweats right down to her ankles. Now there were two full moons shining brightly on this wonderful summer night. One was really white. It could've used a little exposure to the sun!

"Would you look at that!" I exclaimed. Beef and I knelt down to get a much closer look. Several tourists walking past, enjoying a nice stroll on the beach, were just as surprised as Beef and I. The site of Annie bent over underneath a streetlight was pretty shocking, to be sure! Annie didn't wear underwear either...

"Boy, what a design," Beef pointed out. "Very good. You can see everything can't ya?"

"Yes, it's very defined," I said, observing every aspect of the display, "and the tattoo isn't that shabby either!"

"Right, the tattoo..." Beef muttered. He looked at the artwork on her pale left "cheek" and studied it as intently as an archeologist going through a pile of fossils. "What is it?"

"Why it's a rose if I'm not mistaken," I answered.

"Yep, it's a rose!" Annie clarified, still bent over. "I designed it myself!"

"And what a lovely rose it is too!" I said. "What's that? Is that supposed to be a thorn?"

"Uh... that's a hair!" Beef said. He plucked the little hair and Annie let out a small yelp. She turned back around and pulled her sweats back up. She started babbling again, but Beef and I didn't here a word of it. After an eternity, Annie said she had to check on Ripper and wished us a good night. We complimented her on the tattoo and went back to fishing.

"That was different!" Beef said as we settled back in our lawn chairs.

"Yes it was," I said, "but you realize that no one is going to believe this little tale, don't you?"

Beef nodded. Shortly thereafter Wally and The Squirrel came back from their food run.

"Catch anything while we were gone?" Wally asked.

"Just a catfish," Beef answered.

"Any size to it?" Wally questioned.

"Nope," I said. "It was rather petite!"

"Something happened," The Squirrel said, "Beef's drooling!"

Beef was trying to relay the sordid details of Annie's display when I noticed that she was coming back down the pier. Beef and I needed proof of this event. This time, she was coming back empty handed, however. After what was becoming a routine slip and fall off the pier, I helped Annie back up and asked her if she needed something more to drink.

"Oh yesh," she exclaimed. "Got any wine?"

"Hey Wally? You got that bottle of 'Ol' Wallace' in your car?" I asked.

"Yeah . . . you want it?" he offered. I nodded my head and he retrieved the bottle from the trunk. "Ol' Wallace" is Wally's famous homemade apple cider wine. It packs so much of a punch that it can't be truly considered just a wine. The alcohol content is such that if the ATF got a hold of it, it would be deemed a controlled substance in no time! Wally never imbibes alcohol yet one of his hobbies is winemaking. Go figure!

"Here you go," he said as he handed me the bottle. "This ones been aged . . . should have some bite!"

"Ooh, vintage last year!" I gleefully pointed out. Before I could warn Annie about it, she swiped the bottle from my hand and started chugging it down. She polished off half the bottle and began swaying back and forth.

"My tummies all warm," she mumbled as her eyes rolled back in her head.

SMACK! There she lay on the concrete. The Squirrel's mouth dropped open.

"Is she dead?" he asked.

"Wow!" Annie yelled. "That's got shome kick to it!"

Wally and Beef helped Annie back on her feet.

"Say Annie," I said sensing an opportunity, "I'll bet my friends would love to see your tattoo!"

Wally and The Squirrel gave me a confused look and mouthed, "Huh?"

"You think sho?" she whispered.

"Oh yeah!" Beef jumped in. Annie turned around, bent over and down came the sweat pants again. Right down to the ankles as she did before. This time she started stumbling backwards toward Wally.

"Shee it?" she cooed, still stumbling backwards. "Look at it! Ain't it pretty?"

"Holy moly!" Wally gasped, wiping sweat from his brow and backing away. Annie teetered for a moment and then toppled over into the sand. She was out cold, knees spread far apart, sweat pants still around her ankles. Several tourists wandered by on their moonlight strolls and their eyes jumped right out of the sockets.

"Gorgeous night isn't it folks?" Wally nervously conversed. "Boy, look at all those stars . . . don't look down there, look up there . . . in the sky! *Look in the sky!*"

"Nice diversionary tactic," I said. "What are we gonna do now?"

"First, we gotta get her pants back up!" Wally exclaimed. Another round of people wandered by. "We can't leave her here like this!"

"Why not?" The Squirrel asked.

"Yes sir, folks . . . enjoying this fine night are you?" Wally continued. "Nothing like an innocent, uneventful walk on the beach to get the blood pumping! Just keep walking . . . yes sir. Gorgeous night!"

"I can't get her pants back up!" I pointed out. "Too much dead weight!"

"Hurry up!" Wally hissed. Annie would mumble occasionally. "Let me lift her up a little bit, that should help take some weight off! Heh heh, folks... not what it looks like! Just look at the light reflect off that water... breath taking huh? Romantic..."

Beef and The Squirrel, meanwhile, were playing rock, paper, scissors to see who was going to claim this "gift from heaven" as The Squirrel called it.

"Ha, paper beats rock! I win!" Beef shouted.

"That's no fair," The Squirrel squealed. "You got the last one!"

"Knock it off you two!" Wally scolded in his "fatherly" voice. "Have some decency will ya?"

"He's right, Beef," The Squirrel reasoned. "Sharing would be the decent thing to do!"

"*Share?*" Wally erupted, "*Why don't you try having some morals!*"

"I'd thought about having some oral," Beef said, "but with her being passed out and all, I didn't think she'd be..."

"He said 'morals', Beef!" I grunted through clenched teeth, placing strict emphasis on the letter "m" and quickly derailing his simple yet one tracked mind. "*Morals!*"

I finally got Annie's pants back up. She mumbled through her "Ol' Wallace" induced stupor and continued to lie in the sand. The four of us regained our composure and settled back in our lawn chairs, oblivious to the drunken woman immediately behind us. We were fairly calm when, suddenly, the metal walkway on the pier started shaking. The shaking was getting louder and we noticed a large man plodding towards us. He was a really large man... he looked like the Incredible Hulk, only his hair was longer and he was uglier. It was Ripper and, from the looks of things, his anger management activities were unsuccessful. He came off the pier and noticed his girlfriend lying in the sand.

"Aw, Damn it, Annie!" he roared. *"I told ya not to get drunk!"*

Ripper gave us an evil look; we innocently shrugged our shoulders as he hoisted Annie over one shoulder. He carried her to his truck, flopped her in the front seat and tore out of the parking lot. I caught a glimpse of his bumper sticker that read "Guns don't kill people . . . I kill people!"

"That guy was huge!" The Squirrel stated. "What were you thinking, Beef?"

"You know what's funny?" I said. "Just imagine how mad he'd be if she woke up and said something about how we liked her tattoo!"

"That'd be hilarious!" Beef laughed. "If we hear war drums, we'd better get out of here!"

Later that evening as we were fishing along and chuckling over the Annie event, Ripper was busy putting his drunken mate to bed. His mood was most foul at her state of inebriation and what she mumbled next sent him over the edge.

"Those guys were nice," she mumbled. "They really liked my tattoo."

Many miles away, Wally sat up in his lawn chair.

"Did you hear that?" Wally asked. "It sounded like a roar!"

"I didn't hear anything," I said. "How about you guys?"

"Nothing," Beef answered.

"Maybe I'm just getting tired," Wally sighed.

Had there been war drums, we might've had ample warning. Instead we were completely off guard when Ripper's pick up truck screeched into the parking lot and jumped the curb heading straight towards us. We did the brave thing and scattered in all directions when he jumped from the truck, picked up a large piece of driftwood, and charged after us. I won't go into explicit details because there's nothing that I can add to the graphic accounts that showed up in the local newspaper the next day. They were pretty much dead on although they discreetly left out the part about Beef diving into the back seat of some car where two individuals, male and female, were taking advantage of the evening's romantic ambiance. It was probably for the best as I'm sure the young woman's parents would've been shocked to read that their daughter was running around the parking lot without her shirt on let alone the details of how she got to that point! Witnesses were able to describe our panic in full detail. There was the usual screaming, the profanity and the endless fleeing and eluding. They recalled the madman chasing each of us all over hell and back, our dive off the end of the pier and the surprise attack as we tried to sneak to shore.

When Ripper swung the driftwood "club" at Beef's leg and it flew out of his hand due to water, our blood or some other slimy substance, people walking along the beach perfectly quoted my brilliant idea, which for the record, was one of those ideas that's better left unsaid.

"Why the hell are we running? *There's freakin' four of us and only one of him!*" I screamed. The Squirrel took my observation to heart and launched his meek frame onto Ripper's back as the mad man was scrambling around for another piece of wood. Beef and I each grabbed a leg and Wally, reserved under *most* circumstances, stood in front screaming, "*You want a piece of me?*" while dancing around like Sugar Ray Leonard.

The resulting fracas, brought on by a collective display of foolish bravado, began in the parking lot, continued through the putt putt golf course and crashed into a sophisticated outdoor gala on the patio of the Oscoda Area Yacht Club. Several men in black ties valiantly attempted to break up the lengthy skirmish while other Yacht Club members tried to continue with their ballroom dancing. The band kept playing "It Had To Be You" and the members were, understandably, a little miffed at the whole riot. I think that they were mostly

THE FISH OF A THOUSAND CASTS

upset that The Squirrel had mistakenly shattered a bottle of Dom Perignon '65 over Beef's head as I was trying to drown Ripper, or someone with long hair, in a bowl of their fine Beluga caviar. The broken chairs and tables didn't seem to upset them as much as the busted bottle of champagne. Beef, thinking that Ripper had assaulted him with the bottle, returned serve and started bludgeoning away with a turkey leg that he'd grabbed from the scattered remains of the buffet table.

"You like that? Huh? You want some more?" Beef yelled. "I'll give ya some more!"

"Ouch!" Wally screamed. "Who's hitting me with a damn turkey leg? *You want a piece of me? Motherf—!*" Oops, I think the bad influence struck again.

Once the dust had settled and the effects of the pepper spray had worn off, we were able to look back on the evening's festivities with a clear head.

"You gonna call your wife and tell her what happened?" I asked Wally.

"What for . . . she'll just blame you," he answered. "Besides, I think I've got enough money to make bail!"

"Me too," I said.

"Got any idea what a fine for disturbing the peace might run?" Wally asked.

"Oh a hundred," I guessed, "maybe a hundred fifty . . . can't be that much."

"Do you think they'll take credit cards?" Wally questioned.

"I think so," I answered. "I mean, this is a tourist town . . . why wouldn't they?"

Wally and I began to laugh. That's the thing with Wally and I, we can always find the humor in just about anything. We could afford to laugh because *unlike* Beef and The Squirrel, we weren't sharing our holding cell with a mad man named Ripper!

"Maybe if the screaming stops, we can get a little shut eye," I said.

"Uh huh... maybe," Wally sighed.

"Knock off all that screaming, down there!" I shouted down the hall. "Some of us are trying to sleep!"

Big Red

These days it appears that everyone connected with any type of outdoor recreation is driving a fancy SUV. I can't be excluded from that group because I started driving one a couple of years ago. I wouldn't be caught dead in the woods without my beloved Ford Explorer and I know a lot of people who feel the same way about their particular rig. The Sport Utility Vehicle has completely changed the mindset of those who hunt and fish. Its very presence has taken jobs away from those other fine vehicles that used to fill the void.

It hasn't been that long since SUV referred to an entirely different vehicle. Years ago, the SUV was *any* vehicle used to carry guns, tents, boats, coolers, fishing poles, canoes, lanterns, sleeping bags, and worm buckets. In fact, the term SUV hadn't been invented yet. It didn't matter if it was a Pacer, if it was used to carry any of the above mentioned items then it fell under the generic term "Hunting And Fishing Vehicle" or HAFV.

My first HAFV was a '78 Chevy extended van. The first thing I did was remove all the seats in the rear and construct bunk beds and cabinets. That ol' rust bucket was transformed into a fine "mini mobile home" when I was through with it. My friends and I experienced many a good time in the outdoors with that beast of a bus; no matter what condition the road or two-track, it found a way to get us to our destination. Its one draw back, however, was the fact that it was a slight liability when it came to attracting members of the opposite sex. I'm sure you can imagine the look on the young ladies faces when my "gang" and I would roll up to the local beach in the "Sex Mobile" (at least that's what the ladies called it). In hindsight, I can see their skepticism when I tried to explain that the beds were used for sleeping while on fishing expeditions! Maybe it was the bumper sticker that said, "If the van's a rockin' don't come knockin'", that aroused their suspicions...

Since I was fresh out of high school and enjoyed a particular fondness for the female species, I sadly felt that it was in my best interest to change rides. My next vehicle, an '84 Dodge Daytona, cemented my status as a swinging bachelor. It also made one heck of an HAFV. That poor car was loaded to the hilt every weekend with assorted fishing and camping equipment. It was subjected to every terrain available in the state of Michigan and it never complained. In some ways it was the finest HAFV that I ever owned: not only did it perform admirably in the outdoors, but it also did an exquisite job in attracting the ladies; a true "Sex Mobile" if ever there was one! I'm positive that my Explorer would qualify as a "babe magnet" but I wouldn't know. My girlfriend, Steph, I'm sure, would have a thing or two to say about it if I tried to find out! A blown engine caused by too many trips into the wild did the Daytona in and I still mourn it's passing to this day...

My father is no stranger to this outdoor vehicle craze either. While he doesn't own an SUV per se', he does own one of those new "Super Trucks". You know the ones with the fancy toppers and Four Wheel Drive? If there isn't a suitable road for him to travel down, he'll make one. Nothing stops him from reaching a camping spot.

Looking back, it was my father's trials and tribulations with outdoor vehicles that taught me what to look for when purchasing a potential HAFV. For example, I remember the old white truck that he had when I was a youngster. That vehicle was a source of great entertainment for my friends and I. During the last few years of its life starting it was an adventure and my father always reacted in the same fashion. At our age who needed cable TV? My friends and I would simply choose prime locations near the vehicle and wait for my dad to come out and try to start it. Sometimes the truck would tease and start right up, but in the end it would always provide us with enough of a spectacle to satisfy our entertainment dollar. Its favorite routine was the drive 10 feet and stall trick. Boy, if that didn't get my father going nothing would! We'd ooh and ah at my father's fluency in filth like spectators at a 4th of July fireworks display.

When it came to being an outdoors vehicle, it was more than adequate. It hauled our canoes effectively and kept the stalling to a minimum. That truck seemed to have a sixth sense about outdoors excursions. It would run like a top during those, but seemed to be quite rebellious when it came to mundane things like going to work or school. In that respect, I suppose it should be commended. Good upbringing like that in a vehicle is hard to come by in this day and age.

When I was still in elementary school, my family was a one-car unit. The one car in question was a flashy Chevy Camaro. It was pleasing to the eyes but not very effective as an HAFV so my dad needed a vehicle that could handle his outdoor requirements. Money was tight for mom and dad back then and the family budget wouldn't allow anything close to the type of ride that dad *really* wanted. I'll never forget the day he rolled up to the curb in his "new" chariot and forever damaged my perception of an HAFV.

It was an old Chevy Nova, year unknown. The car sported a fresh coat of bright red paint to conceal the start of numerous rust spots. The paint job looked like an abstract artist with a fire hose had applied it. There were no distinguishing stripes or detail work and the rims were a plain black. The interior was equally unsightly as the remnants of the upholstery was held together by various forms of tape, namely duct, masking, and scotch. My father smiled proudly. My mother shuddered with disgust. You know a car has problems when it's given a nickname right off the bat; this rig would be forever known as "Big Red".

Big Red's sole reason for being in the Hutchins house was to provide my father with a facsimile of an HAFV. He immediately began outfitting the car for that very purpose by installing a set of medieval canoe racks. These archaic utensils added a touch of character to Big Red and signaled to the world that this was, indeed, an outdoor vehicle.

Some heavy-duty rubber floor mats were installed to cover the holes in the floor and the upholstery was given a fresh application of duct tape. Slowly I began to grow quite fond of Big Red.

As an HAFV, Big Red lived up to expectations. It hauled canoes with suprising efficiency and had more than enough room to haul the needed camping equipment for a weekend in the wild. It was almost like my father and I had discovered a newfound freedom. Want to go fishing? *NO PROBLEM!* Throw your gear in Big Red! Canoeing? Hunting? Camping? *Big Red can handle it!*

Big Red was our ticket to endless outdoor adventures. My dad knew it, I knew it, and worst of all . . . the car knew it. It wasn't very long before Big Red acquired an attitude.

The car started out with simple demands. If it felt that my father was using motor oil that wasn't up to the standards befitting such a car, it would leak it all over the street and refuse to start until my father replaced it with a better quality grade. My father, ever willing to appease Big Red's idiosyncrasies, would oblige and pump only the finest motor oil into the sputtering remains of the engine.

As Big Red's prima donna attitude expanded so did its demands. In an almost diva like way, it refused to perform until it was satisfied. My father wasn't about to let a dilapidated old car run him into the ground so he refused to honor Big Red's requests. This only infuriated the car and lead to what's now referred to as "Irreconcilable Differences".

The war of words between my dad and the car started out as a minor squabble but soon escalated into a full-blown conflict. Each would insult the other like an old married couple and before long it appeared that the car was gaining the upperhand. My mother and I were innocent bystanders in this war of wills but I suspect my mother found the whole spectacle quite entertaining.

My father's tolerance of the egomaniacal Big Red was uncharacteristic of him but his patience was waning. It only took one major event for Big Red's fate to be sealed.

One hot July day, my dad and I had spent a wonderful afternoon canoeing a local millpond. He wasn't much of a fisherman but he allowed me to fish to my hearts content while he enjoyed the refreshment of a famous adult beverage. When it was time to pack up for the day the car had an attitude.

"Don't even think about throwing that heavy thing up there!" Big Red chastised. "Do you have any idea how freakin' hot it is today? You could have at least parked me in the shade!"

"I'm not in the mood" my father mumbled as he lifted one end of the canoe onto the top of the car. Big Red couldn't be contained. It could dish out a dose of nastiness with the best of them!

"I know, parking me in the shade is just too much of an

inconvenience isn't it? Then you'd have to walk an extra ten freakin' feet to get to your precious freakin' water... and what's with this cheap gas your buying lately? I ask for Perrier and I get tap water!" The car continued to complain as we loaded the paddles and fishing poles in the back seat. My dad was clearly losing his patience when he got behind the wheel and tried to start the car.

WHHHRRRRRR—Click! WHHHRRRRRR—Click!

"I'm not going anywhere until I'm good and ready," Big Red stated. "I was just starting to enjoy this sun!"

My father exploded and I won't even attempt to put his reaction into words. Suffice to say, about the only thing that I can repeat and still avoid an NC-17 rating are the words "car", "piece", and "junkyard".

Big Red was unmoved and, stifling a yawn, said: "That may be my dear fellow but in the interim, *WE AIN'T GOIN' NO FREAKIN' WHERE UNTIL I'M GOOD AND READY!*"

The battle was on and it wasn't pretty. My father shouted insults and expletives and Big Red tossed them right back. When words didn't have any effect, Dad resorted to physical violence. He charged toward the front of the car and violently raised the hood. Big Red, not to be outdone, dropped the hood onto my father's head. Dad bellowed with rage and grabbed the nearest thing he could find, a screwdriver! I ran for cover as the battle carried on and from the distance I watched as my dad, wielding the screw driver like Norman Bates in the famous "shower scene", shoved it into Big Red's carburetor and applied a generous portion of starting fluid. To say the least, the car was not pleased.

"You can't do this to me!" it shouted. "Hutchins! Do you hear me!? *Noooooooooo!*"

My father turned the key and the engine sputtered to life. Big Red, spitting and sputtering its way back to the house, had challenged my father for the last time. My dad's protruding eyes, foaming drool, and noticeable twitch made it apparent

THE FISH OF A THOUSAND CASTS

that there was going to be a change in his method of transportation. He didn't say a word all the way home and I wasn't about to ask him any questions. I certainly had no intentions of intervening on Big Reds behalf either. I know what it's like to get on my father's bad side and the car had definitely crossed the line.

As I stood on the side of the curb in front of our house, sucking on a Popsicle, the car seemed to realize that it had gone on its last adventure.

"Hey Kid, C'mere!" it said with a touch of regret in its voice. "Ya know, I always liked you. What ya say ya give ol' Red a nice drink of that fine oil in the garage? You know... for old times sake?"

I shook my head with such vigor that some drops of Popsicle juice hit the side of the car.

"Oh, so you're spitting on Big Red huh? Heh heh—that's all right—I'm willing to overlook it for a swig of that oil."

I shook my head again as the tow truck from the local junkyard backed up to the front of the car.

"So this is how it ends?" the car began pleading. *"Even death row inmates get a last meal!"*

As the wrecker hitched up to Big Red and started up the street, there were mixed emotions all around. I felt a slight portion of guilt for not granting its last wish, my father saluted Big Red with a visible obscene gesture, and my mother danced a jig around the front yard in celebration of the eyesores departure.

Big Red, of course, was defiant till the end.

"You'll never find a better car than me!" it shouted from the distance. *"NEVER!"*

Of course, Big Red was wrong. The SUV market has so many different vehicles that you could find the perfect one for every sport. I wouldn't trade my Explorer for the world let alone for a car like Big Red; yet, strange as it seems, quite a few of my fondest childhood memories involve the times I spent with my father and . . . that car. My Dad claims to have no recollection of Big Red and it's probably for the best as I would hate to have him relive such a traumatic experience. He can afford to buy any type of fancy outdoor vehicle he wants now and since he recently purchased the newest, high tech, "Next Best Thing In An Outdoors Vehicle", I would hate to disrupt his euphoria with a reminder of Big Red.

As for me, Big Red will always have a place in my memories. I can't think of the days spent fishing and canoeing with The Chief without being reminded of that car. Rust in peace Big Red. Rust in peace . . .

My Days at Camp Happi-Sissie

The last few hours of 5th grade were winding down. The blessed parole of summer vacation was just around the corner and the time was barely moving. Most of us had already turned in our schoolbooks and the day was simply utilized for social activities and locker cleaning. It was bittersweet. Normally, we children couldn't wait for summer break but this year was different. Never again would we terrorize the fine staff at Mauck Elementary School. The next fall would be our first in middle school. The end of an era was near.

The school bell rang for the final time. Beef and I slowly departed the playground where we'd spent our entire school life. We quickly remembered all the fun we'd had there and surveyed our territory one last time.

"Ok, now what?" Beef asked.

"Beats me," I answered. "Wanna play some baseball?"

Sentiment wears off quickly when you're only ten years

old. You really don't become sentimental until you're a little older-maybe fifty or sixty.

We had two months of freedom before we took a major step toward adulthood and entered the dreaded middle school. At Mauck, we were the kings of the castle. We spent years establishing our reputations and rising up the pecking order. Now we would have to start over again. Life wasn't fair.

The next week, we prepared for our annual appearance at summer camp. Again, this was bittersweet because it marked our last time there as well.

There were two summer camps in the area. Camp Sleepy Tree and Camp Happi-Sissie. The rich kids in the county got to attend Camp Sleepy Tree; the rest of us in the middle and lower classes bunked at Camp Happi-Sissie. If you ask me, the names should have been switched around. We were anything but "happy sissies" that designation should have been reserved for the spoiled rich punks!

One rich kid, Oliver, spent the last week of school hounding me about how his camp was going to beat my camp in the annual campers olympics. Camp Sleepy Tree had beaten us every year that I was there and this was my last chance to go out a winner . . . and drink from the coveted "Wooden Mug". The wooden mug was a giant mug carved from (you guessed it) wood. It went to the winning camp every year and was on display during the entire camp games. I wanted to drink from that cup just once before I retired from summer camp. Oliver's boasting was a little out of place since he never contributed much to winning it. Every year it came down to one last race between another rich kid, nicknamed Flash, and me. I always came out on the losing end . . . by a hair, mind you. Flash and I were rivals through and through. We always ended up competing against each other in area track meets. Sometimes I'd win, sometimes I'd lose, but at the camp Olympics, I always ended up in 2nd place. I hate second place and reminded Oliver of that fact with a swift beating.

THE FISH OF A THOUSAND CASTS

"Do what you want," he said, "but we're still going to keep the mug."

There is nothing worse than someone being smug, especially after you've just beaten the tar out of them!

It was a Friday when my mother dropped Beef and I off at Camp Happi-Sissie. She imparted us with a simple warning about "how she better not get a phone call from the counselor's like last year," and we began our final appearance at summer camp.

The counselors were the same as last year. Clarence, a hypochondriac who's allergic to everything; Todd, the local body builder; Russell, the know it all; Betty, the camp nurse; Melinda, the object of everyone's desires; Alice, the rough and tumble ex-shot put champion; and Mr. Steele, the Head Counselor who welcomed Beef and I back with open arms.

"If you idiots try the (insert expletive here) you tried last year, I'll personally see to it that you both suffer incredible discomfort!" stated Mr. Steele.

It's nice to know that certain misdeeds will never be forgotten. I like having a feeling of notoriety. Heck, I know for a fact that my 5th grade teacher will never forget me! But I digress . . .

Todd, the body builder, was our counselor and we were assigned cabin # 4. There were five of us in the cabin. It was the same cast of characters as last year with one exception. A new kid with braces and a slight over bite who was extremely scrawny. Beef, Dave "The Mumbler" Gibbs, Buddy Lumpkins, the new kid (we never caught his name), and myself were quite a rough bunch to be sure. We made an agreement that since this was the last year for us, we were going to see to it that cabin # 4 would go down in the annals of Camp Happi-Sissie history.

By nature, I'm usually the most outgoing of any group so I unofficially assumed the role of cabin leader. The main goal I set forth was to attain the celebrated Wooden Mug, but there were fun and activities to enjoy first. The camp olympics would take care of themselves later.

The first day at camp was spent getting reacquainted with everyone. Most of the kids attended different elementary schools so the only time you saw anyone was at summercamp. The first activity of camp was the famed "stream stomp".

I really enjoyed the stream stomp. It was one of my favorite activities that involved putting on a pair of old sneakers and walking up and down a stream collecting water bugs, rocks, frogs and anything nature related. The purpose of such an activity was to teach us about the aquatic life cycle and certain species that reside in area streams. That part was lost on us. In our eyes, it was merely an excuse to get your shoes wet without having to worry about retribution from an angry mother!

As we all tromped up and down the stream, Clarence, the hypochondriac counselor, was whining incessantly about his allergies and barking at his troop of campers to stop stirring up so much pollen. Todd used the outing as an excuse to take his shirt off and flex his muscles for Melinda. Alice, the shot put champion was showing her group of girls the fine art of the shot put using various rocks. Russell spewed forth his vast knowledge of everything and explained the importance of each creature. Betty, the camp nurse, was waiting in the wings with a salt shaker to remove any leeches that had made their way onto our legs.

Beef and I were trying to chase down a crayfish when *she* caught my eye . . .

Her name was Maggie and she was a sweet young girl from another elementary school. I was at that age when girls were no longer the enemy and the awkwardness of being infatuated with them was starting to take hold. Maggie gave me a cute little smile and I did my best Paul Stanley impression and blew her a kiss. At the time, Paul Stanley, of the rock group KISS, was my idol and I tried to imitate his every move.

He was quite popular with the ladies you know. Maggie blushed a little bit and blew me a kiss right back. I couldn't take my eyes off her and as I kept walking I didn't notice the big rock at my feet. Boy, was I suave when I tripped over that rock and landed face first in the cool stream. I jumped up as quickly as I could and Maggie giggled and rejoined her group.

"Paul Stanley wouldn't do that," Beef said. "Good thing you didn't pull a Gene Simmons and stick out your tongue!"

"I think she likes me!" I answered with water dripping off my nose. I sighed that young puppy love type sigh and went about my business of capturing the crayfish.

The evening was spent around a huge campfire and everyone sang songs and toasted marshmallows. I made my way over to Maggie and struck up a conversation.

"Uh... like... what's up... I mean... uh... Hi!" I smoothly said. We Hutchins men are suave.

"Hi!" Maggie answered. "My names Maggie, what's yours?"

"Uh... Uh... Uh..." I couldn't remember my own freaking name! Finally I got hold of myself and blurted out: "Stef!"

"Stef? That's a weird name," she said.

Stef? What in the world was that? I was sinking fast. They simply don't teach the art of talking to girls in school. How is a young lad like me supposed to deal with the complexity of interacting with the opposite sex if you don't have an instruction book or something!

"Wanna share a marshmallow?" Maggie offered.

I nodded my head and she handed me a marshmallow to toast. I burned it of course but she didn't mind. That marshmallow was the most enjoyable I ever had in my life. I really liked that little girl. As the activities wound down for the evening, Maggie said goodnight to me and blew me a kiss as she walked away. In a daze, I wandered around the campground thinking of her.

"Hey Hutchins!" Todd blurted out. "The cabins this way..." he grabbed me by the shirt and led me to the cabin. When we were back in the cabin, Todd laid out the rules for the night.

"I'm going to be out for awhile... uh... stargazing... understand?" Todd said. "That means you guys better behave yourselves and go to sleep. I don't want Mr. Steele coming over here and finding me gone... got it?"

We nodded our heads. We knew what Todd meant by stargazing, we weren't that young and dumb. There was a well-known myth among the younger campers about a ghost that roams the camp. Sometimes at night, you could hear its moans and groans echo through the woods. Well, since we were growing up in the early stages of HBO, us older kids knew what the ghost really was! The only time the ghost made an appearance was when Todd was out "stargazing". Todd seemed to make a habit of "stargazing" with Melinda and let's just say that their "stargazing" activities were rather loud! We could hear the younger kids in another cabin panic as the strange groans began filling the air. Us older kids giggled and cracked jokes.

"There goes that ghost again!" Dave said.

"Boy, I hope it doesn't get Todd," Beef answered with a touch of sarcasm.

"I think it's too late..." I said. We laughed ourselves to sleep as the eerie moans slowly faded into the night...

The week was going by rather fast. There were lots of fun activities to enjoy like canoeing, fishing, swimming, craftwork (I hated that) and archery. I was pretty good with a bow. When your father is known as The Chief, you kind of pick up things like archery and canoeing with relative ease. The new kid in our cabin didn't say much. He had to wear one of those head gear things for his braces and it rendered him a little sloppy in his speech. He just went along with the rest of us but stayed pretty quiet. Maggie and I continued

THE FISH OF A THOUSAND CASTS

our playful flirtations and the ghost made numerous appearances at night. I'll say this, those ghosts certainly have a lot of stamina!

At long last, the camp Olympics drew near. In cabin # 4 we schemed and plotted a course of action should we not win the wooden mug. I know you never plan for failure, but we wanted to have all our bases covered on this one. The rich brats were not going to get the upper hand on us again. Even if they had the mug, they were still going to pay!

"We need to do something that they'll remember forever!" I said.

"What about poison ivy in their sleeping bags?" Buddy suggested.

"Did that last year . . . didn't work, got it all over our hands, remember?" Beef said. "I itched for a week!"

"How about greasing up their canoe paddles?" Dave offered.

"They're rich . . . why would they need canoe paddles?" I said. "They probably have someone to paddle for them."

"It's simple," Buddy added, "if they win the mug, we just beat the crap out of them like at school!"

"Well . . . I do like that idea," I said. "Since this is our last year here, they can't ban us!"

"Alright then!" Dave said. "It's settled. We'll just beat 'em up real good!"

Finally, out of nowhere, the new kid spoke up.

"I have a better idea," he said with a severe lisp. His braces and headgear caused him to have an odd speech impediment. We gathered around the new kid as he explained all the details of his plan. It was so ingenious that we couldn't help but get excited. When he was finished explaining, we all agreed that his was the best plan to implement.

"Ok, we're all in agreement on this," I said, "but remember, we only do this if we're in a dire situation and it looks like we won't win the mug!"

The next day, everyone from both camps gathered in a neutral area for the start of the games. There were tents set up for each camp and a big score board that would show the results for every event.

The first event was the obstacle course. Competitors would have to race through a series of obstacles, climb way up a tree and swing from a rope to another tree. There, they would grab a flag, climb back down and sprint toward the finish line. The new kid was chosen to represent our cabin in this event. Since he was so scrawny, we figured he could wiggle through the obstacles with little effort. We were right!

The gun sounded and the new kid lead the pack from the very beginning. He conquered each obstacle like they weren't even there and when he reached the first tree we were simply amazed. He was almost animal like as he scooted up the side of the tree and bounced from branch to branch with an uncanny resemblance to a bushy tailed, buck toothed creature.

"Look at that!" Beef said. "He looks just like a squirrel!"

"Yes he does," I said.

And that became the new kids nickname. From there on out, he was forever known as The Squirrel.

After one event, the scoreboard showed Camp Happi-Sissie in the lead.

The next event was the canoe race. Beef and I would represent our cabin in this. My reputation for handling a canoe was well known so we were assured a victory. I looked over at the canoe next to us and Oliver gave me an evil look. That's just how I like it. Not only did I physically beat him up, but I was going to whip him in the canoe race as well.

"Ready . . . Set . . . Go!"

We dug our canoe paddles into the water and shot off the starting line. Just as the canoes were launching, Oliver dipped his paddle deep into the water and unleashed a splash that covered my face and temporarily blinded me. With water in my eyes, I inadvertently steered us away from the course.

THE FISH OF A THOUSAND CASTS

When I finally got my bearings, Oliver's canoe was out in front by a hefty margin.

"What are you doing!" Beef shouted. "Get us back on track!"

"Just dig in!" I shouted back. "I'm going to get that little..."

Beef and I paddled like the wind and swiftly gained on the rich kid's canoe. They had no idea the thoughts that were going through my mind but appeared panic stricken when they noticed our canoe zoning in on them at ramming speed. I dug my paddle into the water with the intensity of a vengeance-craving madman!

"Look out!" Oliver screamed. "You can't do that!"

WHAM! Beef and I slammed into the side of Oliver's canoe with such force that it knocked them off course and forced them to do a big circle. We continued through the course and won by a huge advantage.

As Oliver's canoe pulled back to shore, I chased after him and got quite a few licks in before the counselors could break it up. A huge brawl ensued in the aftermath and it looked like one of those bench clearing baseball skirmishes. There was no love lost between the camps and even the counselors got involved! Maggie came up and told me how brave I was and planted a small kiss on my cheek. I fainted. When I woke up, I found myself staring at the snarling face of Mr. Steele.

"I could really let you have it for starting that little brawl!" he said. "But I'm not going to. Do what you have to do... I want that mug! I'm tired of coming in second place to that camp!" He helped me up and gave me a pat on the back.

After all the events of the day, our camp was slightly in front of the rich kid's camp on the scoreboard. We won most of the physical events, but they really cleaned up in the other artsy events like craft making. There wasn't much conversation around the campfire that evening. The mission was clear and the mug was within our reach.

"Remember . . . plan B only goes into effect if something dire happens and it looks like all hope is lost!" I reminded my cabin mates.

The next morning didn't go well for our camp. We were beaten in several events that we should have won and Camp Sleepy Tree jumped ahead in the standings. As their enthusiasm grew, ours withered.

"Is it time for plan B yet?" Buddy asked.

"Not yet," I said, "it's not over yet."

After lunch, our camp regrouped and we started mounting a valiant comeback. Timmy smoked the competition in the swimming event and Maggie proved to be quite a shot in the girl's archery shoot. The Squirrel once again came through in the second obstacle course. I was mostly a spectator. I had to save my energy for the last event: the Dash Through The Woods.

The games wound to a finish and both camps were tied. As always, it came down to that last event.

There was silence from both camps as Flash and I approached the starting blocks. Beef and the rest of my gang were nowhere to be found. Everyone, except my gang, gathered around the finish line. They had witnessed the fierce battles between Flash and I at numerous track meets and they knew they were in for a doozy this time. Last event at the last year of camp and it was all for the glory of the wooden mug. What could be better than that? Mr. Steele looked over at me and mouthed the words; "I want that cup". Flash glanced my way and nodded his head in salute to our competitive nature. I nodded back. You always have some element of respect for your rivals.

The event was simple. A make shift track was set up and wound through the woods to the finish line 200 yards away. The rules were equally simple: run as fast as you can! I was going to be the goat or the hero. Time stood still as we crouched in the starting position. There were other kids

THE FISH OF A THOUSAND CASTS

involved besides Flash and I, but they were simply filler. Everyone knew it was about us.

Finally, after what seemed like an eternity, the gun sounded and the event was underway. Flash and I left the rest of the kids in our dust and raced neck and neck for quite a distance. The finish line was getting closer and closer as Flash starting breaking away from me. Frustration filled my head as it appeared that he was going to vanquish me yet again. I saw my last chance for swigging from the coveted mug slipping away. Mr. Steele covered his face with his hands. The agony of losing to the other camp again started to take hold. Flash was a couple steps ahead of me and I couldn't gain. The finish line was so close...

I broke my concentration and my eyes drifted over to the side of the track. I saw Maggie as she was urging me on. I dug deep into my being and conjured up another gear. I gained on Flash very quickly. We were neck and neck once again. He glanced over at me and I could see it in his face. Fear. He knew that I was going to beat him! I kept digging and was half a step ahead. I thrust forward with everything I had and crossed the finish line in front! My camp erupted in cheers!

Maggie ran up as everyone was patting me on the back and gave me a tight bear hug. Todd picked me up with his massive arms and carried me over to the table that housed the famed wooden mug.

The mug was crude. A simple chalice carved from an old log, it didn't look very appealing but the symbolism of it meant more than words can say. I held it in my hand for the first time and the rush of emotions cannot be described. I turned around and held it high for everyone in the camp to see. I was just getting ready to take the drink that I so longed for when I noticed my gang assembled off to the side.

Beef, Dave, Buddy and The Squirrel stood with mouths wide open as I prepared to gulp from the wooden mug. Simultaneously, they shook their heads as if to say, "Don't do it!" I knew right then and there that while they were absent from the dash, they were implementing plan B.

Everyone from my camp began chanting "Drink! Drink! Drink!" Beef kept shaking his head but what choice did I have? I had to drink.

The mug was just about to touch my lips when Mr. Steele rushed up and swiped it from my hands.

"Oh no you don't!" he stated. "I've waited a long time for this moment!"

He took the mug and began gulping the precious liquid that it held. He drank until it was empty and never noticed the funny taste I'm sure it had as a result of plan B.

"The taste of victory!" Mr. Steele triumphantly announced. "How sweet it is!"

I walked over to my cabin mates who stared at me with a look of disbelief.

"Good thing you didn't drink that!" Beef said.

"Why did you guys do that! I thought I said to do it if all hope was lost!" I questioned the group.

"Right," answered Buddy, "you said if all hope was lost—you haven't beaten Flash in that event ... ever!"

"How were we supposed to know you'd win now?" Dave added.

"It looked hopeless to us," Beef said.

"Thanks for the support!" I said. "At least you warned me before I took a drink of that stuff!"

"I don't want to be around Mr. Steele when that Ex-Lax takes effect," Beef said. "Man, that's gonna hurt!"

And hurt it did. As all the Happi-Sissie campers gathered around the fire for one last time, it was a celebration. A jovial gathering to celebrate the triumph of winning the wooden mug and to enjoy the company of friends both old and new. Mr. Steele was absent from the party but was present in spirit. You could hear him as the most hideous and nerve-shattering screams emanated from one of the outhouses. In between screams he'd repeatedly announce his intent to exact vengeance upon those responsible for his current state of extreme discomfort.

"I know who's responsible for this!" he agonized. "I will get you for this!"

And the hideous screams would begin again...

Bright and early the next morning, all the parents were waiting to take the camper's home. Beef and I took one last look at the campground and hastily said our good-byes. I promised to call Maggie during the summer and asked if she would be my girl friend when we got to middle school—she said she would. I wasn't in any position for a long goodbye and she understood the reasons why. Mr. Steele, looking frail, gaunt, and much thinner, was stalking the campground. He finally caught sight of Beef and I and started rushing towards us. We ran over to my mother's car.

"I didn't get any phone calls this year," she said. "That's good. Maybe you're starting to out grow all those pranks!"

"Summer's just started," I said as I tossed my duffel bag in the backseat. "Can we go now... *please!*"

"Always in a hurry," my mother sighed, "God forbid you might miss something."

We pulled away from the camp and Beef and I nervously looked out the back window. The last thing I'll remember about Camp Happi-Sissie is the image of Mr. Steele chasing the car for over half a mile, waving his fist high in the air.

It was a narrow escape but his vengeance would befall us eventually. That autumn, at middle school, we were introduced to our new Phys Ed teacher. A spiteful, bitter man by the name of... Mr. Steele!

The Ghost of Tripping Beaver

My father, The Chief, was always looking for ways to have fun in the outdoors. It didn't matter if it was back yard camping trips, bonfires, or canoe excursions at the local millpond; the outdoors was our playground. We were always doing something that involved the outdoors . . . it's who we are.

Now, when I speak of this in the past tense, I'm *not* trying to imply that The Chief has passed on to the spirit world. The Chief is alive, well, and still the adventurous one despite the decrepitness of his 60 years of age. It's just that he's slowed down a little in his twilight years. He seems to focus more on his other personality, the globetrotting tourist, than he does his role as The Chief. His outdoor skills are slipping because of it and he's resorting to the very things that he used to ridicule me about.

Take my use of rental cabins for instance. When Beef, Wally and I go north for extended salmon fishing trips, we

THE FISH OF A THOUSAND CASTS

rent a cabin. Why fumble around with a tent when all you want to do is sleep, eat and fish? The cabin is excellent at providing a haven for sleeping and eating, *without* all the inconveniences of a tent. I love camping... but lets face it, camping time is one thing and fishing time is another. Time spent setting up and taking down a camp is time subtracted from fishing. It's all about priorities! The Chief would crack jokes about our choice of shelter and would frequently question our... uh... manhood, until a couple of years ago, that is.

We'd invited him to join us several times and he always had some excuse not to. Finally, my mother intervened and forced him into his vehicle and he found himself knocking on the door of our cabin.

"I'm expected to stay in this?" he questioned. "This is hardly suitable for a world traveler like myself!"

"Yeah, but it's good enough for The Chief," I said. "The Chief doesn't mind a little squalor!"

"I just got back from England chaps," The Chief stated. "I'm not feeling like The Chief yet."

It didn't take long for him to revert back to his outdoor loving persona. By the end of his stay, he'd stopped bad mouthing the cabin and started complimenting its convenience.

"This isn't so bad," He complimented. "Are you going to get a bigger one for next year?"

"Next year?" I asked.

"Yeah, next year," he answered. "I wouldn't miss this for the world! Heck, I might even bring up a couple of my buddies."

He never would have enjoyed a cabin a few years ago. If it wasn't a canvas, mountain man, wall tent or a homemade teepee, then he didn't want any part of it. The Chief has definitely gotten softer as the years creep up on him!

Back when I was younger, The Chief was always building

some sort of Indian lodging. Longhouses, stick huts and teepees were a mandatory part of our camping experiences. No one could build a teepee like The Chief. He'd been building them since he was a kid and his knowledge grew to such a point that even Sitting Bull would be hard pressed to build a better shelter! Whenever The Chief bought a new batch of canvas, a new teepee was to be erected.

When I was just eight years old, The Chief came home one day with his old white truck loaded with two things: a new canoe and a batch of canvas. I grinned from ear to ear when he pulled into the driveway because his new acquisitions meant that a camping and canoeing trip was on the immediate horizon.

"Like her?" The Chief asked as he pointed out the new canoe. "We're going to break her in this weekend!"

"Can Beef come along?" I asked.

"Of course!" The Chief answered. "Tell him to bring his sleeping bag. I figure we'll float down the Muskegon and camp along shore. You guys can do a little fishing while I do some grouse hunting."

"We gonna build a teepee or sleep in a tent?" I questioned.

"Teepee! What do you think the canvas is for?" The Chief said, smiling.

The very next weekend, we loaded the old truck with the necessary equipment and set forth toward the Muskegon River. Beef had recently been battling a severe soar throat and it took some coaxing for his grandmother, who he lived with next door to us, to let him out of the house. To ease his sore throat, she'd mixed up a bottle of some old fashioned "throat tonic". The tonic, which was in a fruit juice bottle, consisted of various, numbing, ingredients and had as much power as liquid novocaine. He'd gargle with that every once in a while and his mouth and throat would be completely numb for hours. He didn't say much on the way to the river and it was probably for the best. The Chief used to get very

THE FISH OF A THOUSAND CASTS

irritated during long drives and having Beef and I in the same vehicle usually didn't help matters. Beef's numb mouth prohibited us from engaging in our usual arguments and verbal highjinks and The Chief was still in a pleasant mood when we got to the river.

With two eight year olds in a canoe, The Chief's mood had started to get a bit foul. I don't know what he was fretting about, it was completely accidental that his beer spilled and we almost tipped over. The weekend we chose for this trip was during a mid-autumn warm spell. Bugs and other creatures took the opportunity during the warm period to tend to last minute business before they went into winter hibernation. A large dragonfly decided to keep landing on the back of my neck and it was very irritating. I didn't realize it was a dragonfly at first and thought it was Beef messing around as he sat behind me on one of the coolers.

"Knock it off, Beef!" I said, swatting at the air behind me.

"Knock what off?" he answered. The novocaine concoction had worn off and he was speaking normally. The Dragonfly buzzed my neck again.

"That!" I shouted. My swatting behind me caused the canoe to start rocking.

"Settle down!" My father barked as the canoe rocked in the swift current. "You're going to tip us over!"

"Tell Beef to knock it off," I whined. The dragonfly made another pass.

"I'm not doing anything!" Beef shouted. I grabbed my fishing pole and swung it behind me in an attempt to whack Beef. He saw it coming and ducked to one side. The canoe then tipped to that side. My father barked some more. Since Beef ducked, the tip of my rod went over his head and connected with The Chiefs hand . . . the one holding the beer. He dropped the beer and it landed in his lap. The dragonfly flew away when The Chief's barrage of foul language filled the tranquil air. He was always getting wound up over little things like that...

That's the thing about The Chief, you can tell when he's angry by the amount of cursing he adds to a sentence. He never, ever, swears during casual conversation, but when he's mad... watch out! Being a student of the Indian culture, he once boasted that he knew how to speak Indian but... it was usually just phrases he heard in a movie. The Pottowattomi were the band of Indians that used to live in the area of Hillsdale county, therefore if The Chief did know any Indian language it would've had to have been pottowattomese. I later deduced that he learned his lingo from a renegade band known as the "Profanitee" tribe. When he was angered he would revert to that lingo and I discovered, at my expense, that he was quite fluent in "profanitese".

My father grew tired of our escapades and quickly located a spot in the woods for setting up camp.

He searched high and low for the best teepee poles possible and erected the frame of our shelter. A large tripod stood 15 feet in the air and he filled in the gaps with several other slender poles. Beef and I watched as he pieced together the dark brown canvas and adjusted the flap that would allow the smoke to escape from the campfire inside. In no time at all, he had it constructed and we laid out our bedding and started the fire. It was one of the finest teepees he'd ever built. The Chief sat back on a log, opened a can of Coke (no beer this time, he was getting ready to hunt) and admired the shelter as it blended nicely with the surrounding forest. You could almost picture the adjacent Indian village and the activity that accompanied it. Beef and I grabbed our trusty Zebco 202's and headed toward the river.

"Stay right in this area!" The Chief advised. "Don't go wandering off. I'm going to try and flush some grouse from that thicket back there."

Beef and I stood on the riverbank, baited our hooks with

THE FISH OF A THOUSAND CASTS

thick leaf worms, and tossed them into the rusty current. That kind of life is wonderful, no matter if you're eight or 80. We managed to get a few decent sized brown trout and threw them on the bank to have for dinner that night. At that stage of our fishing careers "decent sized" meant anything that was bigger than the worm! Our young ears had never heard of catch and release. The Chief was apparently flushing some grouse since we heard a couple of gunshots boom forth from the thicket. This was turning into one of those camping trips that you remember for a lifetime!

Long attention spans are not programmed into boys our age and Beef and I soon grew tired of fishing. We started skipping rocks across the water and began searching the banks for frogs, crayfish and other aquatic creatures. To fuel our creative urges, we attempted to build crude Indian devices. I took a rather limber stick, tied a piece of kite string from one end to another, and had my own homemade version of a bow. Since I had the bow, I needed arrows. The bank we were playing on was loaded with sand stone so I began looking for pieces that resembled arrowheads. Beef found a piece that looked like a tomahawk blade and he tied it to a forked stick. I had the bow, he had the tomahawk, heck, we were pretty mean looking little Indians! I found several rocks that looked like arrowheads and I started scraping them against other rocks to sharpen the points... and I did a mighty fine job of it, I might add. Next, I took a roll of electrical tape out of my little tackle box and taped the arrowheads onto several straight sticks I'd gathered. I notched the ends out so they'd fit in my bowstring. The whole set up didn't look half-bad! Beef was trying to scalp a tree with his new tomahawk and I drew back my bow and aimed toward an old stump. The bow had more power than I thought and the arrow soared right over the stump and into the bushes behind it.

"Help! I'm under attack!" a voice cried out from the bushes.

Beef and I walked through the bushes and saw an elderly gentleman tossing a fly rod from the bank of the river. He had long gray hair tied into a ponytail and a slight wisp of a beard. His kind old eyes lit up when we emerged from the bushes.

"I'll give you your arrow back if you promise not to scalp me!" The gentleman joked, eyeballing Beef's tomahawk.

"Nah, we won't scalp ya!" Beef said. "You don't seem mean."

"Name's Orville," he said, "Orville Lightfeather, what's yours?"

We introduced ourselves and proudly told him that we were "eight years old . . . almost grown up!"

"Lightfeather's a weird last name," I said. "Where'd you get that?"

"It's Chippewa," he answered. "I'm half Indian."

Whoa! A real live Indian? Cool! We'd never met one before! The Chief was the only "Indian" I'd ever met and he was really just a white man who *thought* he was an Indian who *thought* he was a globetrotting playboy (although my mother would chuckle at the latter portion of that statement). We told Mr. Lightfeather about our teepee.

"I saw it," he said, "and what a fine teepee it is."

The Chief came walking up the bank with four grouse stuffed in his game pouch. He introduced himself to Mr. Lightfeather and they began talking about the teepee. Soon after, Mr. Lightfeather invited us to his camp for dinner. We accepted.

Mr. Lightfeather was retired and he'd been camped in the area for a couple of weeks. His campsite was made up of a large wall tent and he had a big fire pit with cooking utensils scattered about. What a life, I thought. I couldn't wait to be retired so I could spend as much time in the outdoors as I wanted.

"If you're an Indian, where's your teepee?" Beef asked.

His sore throat was acting up again and his voice was hoarse. He removed the fruit juice bottle from his jacket, took a gargle of his grandma's homemade novocaine throat tonic and didn't say anything else for quite a while after that.

"I don't know much about teepee building," Mr. Lightfeather explained. "I only know a few Indian tales that my grandfather once told me."

The smell of sizzling trout and grouse was heavenly. Mr. Lightfeather threw in some fried potatoes and corn on the cob. It was probably one of the best dinners I've ever had. As it got darker, some ominous storm clouds appeared on the horizon. As with any of our adventures in the outdoors, the threat of rain has followed Beef and I no matter where we go or what we do!

Once it was dark, we sat around the campfire. The Chief tried to pick Mr. Lightfeather's brain for any Indian knowledge he had. They were enjoying a number of adult beverages . . . and getting quite inebriated in the process. Beef and I toasted marshmallows. The Chief got into the spirit of things by rolling up a handkerchief and tying it around his head like a headband. He stuffed a bunch of tail feathers from the grouse he'd shot into the headband and sat there with a pretty cool looking imitation of an Indian headdress.

"Let me tell you a little tale," Mr. Lightfeather said. All ears turned to attention and the old man started telling his story.

"There's power in these woods," he began, "a power that we'll never understand. A long time ago when the natives ruled this land, a brave by the name of Tripping Beaver was famous throughout the entire Chippewa nation. Tripping Beaver was strong and feared nothing, but he was also a bit clumsy. That's how he came about his name; he was constantly tripping over something. His brothers, Hairy Beaver and Gnawing Beaver, would always pick on him no matter what he did. If he was chasing game, he'd end up tripping over some log or rock and the game would get away! For all his strength, Tripping Beaver was only known for his clumsiness. This angered him something fierce. He couldn't stand being ridiculed."

"Did he kill everyone who picked on him?" I asked.

"Nope, wasn't his style!" Mr. Lightfeather continued. "Tripping Beaver decided to set out on his own and create a nation that didn't pick on him. He wanted to be a chief and that wasn't about to happen . . . living where he was living that is. He loaded his canoe, said goodbye to his brothers, and started down this very river right behind us."

"Was it a birch bark canoe?" The Chief inquired. He was always asking questions like that.

"Yep . . . built it himself!" Mr. Lightfeather said. "He didn't know where he was going, but he knew that this river had to lead somewhere. He canoed for a couple days, and when he came around the bend back there, he saw a deer by the riverbank. Now ol' Tripping Beaver was feeling a little hungry, you see, so he got out his bow and shot the deer! Whack . . . direct hit! And the deer fled into the woods. Tripping Beaver pulled up to shore and followed the blood trail into the forest. Just as he was coming up on where the deer had laid down, he tripped over a big old log . . . might've been that one right there, who knows, but this time it was a nasty fall. Tripping Beaver tried to get back up but his leg was broke and twisted like a pretzel. He couldn't walk and just kinda laid there . . . until it got so cold that he couldn't take it anymore. He cried the old Chippewa war cry and died right then and there!"

"Died?" we all asked, swallowing hard. I clutched my bow and arrows, Beef tightened his hands around his tomahawk and The Chief chuckled at our nervousness and took a few more swigs of his beer.

"Dead as a door knob!" Mr. Lightfeather went on. "But his spirit didn't die with him. You see this forest belongs to

THE FISH OF A THOUSAND CASTS

Tripping Beaver now, and he swore vengeance on anyone who settles here! His spirit wanders around looking for trespassers. Since he was all alone, he didn't receive a proper Indian burial. Now he's doomed to haunt this forest until the end of time! An old trapper saw him once . . . just once, mind you. You never get to see Tripping Beaver's ghost a second time. He finishes the job right quick! Sometimes, when he's mad, you can hear his war cry in the wind. Heck, he's probably watching us at this very moment!"

The wind started rushing through the trees and the sky came alive with the sound of thunder. I felt a slight chill and it gave me goosebumps.

"Storms here," Mr. Lightfeather said amidst flashes of lightening, "or maybe it's ol' Tripping Beaver! *What was that?* Did you see something moving by that tree over there?"

Beef and I were terrified. The Chief finished his last beer and said that it was time to hit the sack.

A few raindrops were hitting the ground and the thunder rumbled like the sound of war drums as we scurried back toward the teepee. Well, Beef and I scurried that is; The Chief was a little slow from his drinking activities. His grouse feather headdress added a little comic effect to his staggering.

"Hurry up, Pop!" I yelled behind me. "The ghost of Tripping Beaver might get us!"

"There's no ghost out here," my father said, "that was just an old Indian tale!"

"Well, I'm ready for Tripping Beaver if he wants to come and gets us!" Beef stated. He swung his tomahawk in the air in a mock display of bravado. "I'll whack him in the head and then you shoot him with an arrow! That'll take care of that ghost!"

"How ya gonna whack a ghost?" I asked. "They're just air. My arrow will go right through like he's not even there! Don't you pay attention to the movies?"

"Uh . . . you're right," Beef said. "I hope that old ghost don't think we're trying to settle here!"

"Mr. Tripping Beaver, sir?" I cried out. "We're just camping here. We'll be gone tomorrow so . . . you just stay away, ok?"

We picked up our pace considerably and made it back to the teepee just as the sprinkles of rain escalated to a torrential down pour.

The glowing embers of our campfire had heated the teepee very well. It was comfortable enough, but Beef and I stayed dressed in our pants. The Chief, feeling the effects of the alcohol no doubt, complained of the heat and stripped all the way down to his underwear. He was so tired that he didn't even take his grouse feather headdress off. Every time he'd snore, the feathers would vibrate. Beef clutched his tomahawk as he fell asleep and I had my bow and arrows within reaching distance. We were very nervous that Tripping Beaver was going to make an appearance . . . the thunder continued to boom.

I don't know how late it was, but at some point The Chief awoke from his stupor and decided that he was very thirsty. He wandered around the teepee in his underwear and grouse feather headdress, looking for something to drink.

"Chief . . . thirsty," he mumbled, smacking his lips. "Ah . . . *fruit juice!*"

In the glow of the campfire, he spotted a bottle of fruit juice sitting on the ground near Beef. He picked up the bottle, removed the cap, and began taking huge gulps. His face began to tingle as he lost all feeling in his mouth and throat. He tried to spit out what was left on his tongue, but he'd already ingested a huge amount of the homemade throat tonic!

"Nod Rammit!" The Chief hissed. His face began to droop and was somewhat disfigured by the sudden loss of muscle control. He looked down at the bottle he was holding in his hand.

"*Dis ids not phluckin' flute joots!*" he exclaimed. It didn't take long for the mixture of beer and throat tonic to throw his stomach into a tizzy. I don't believe that the tonic was ever meant to be swallowed and as a result The Chief became very queasy. His futile grunts and stuttered attempts at "profanitese" soon turned to eerie moans and groans. Beef and I were awakened by a loud thunder crack. What we heard after that, were the moans . . .

"Do y-y-you hear th-th-that?" I whispered. My voice was trembling with fear.

"Y-y-yeah," Beef whispered back. His voice was equally nervous. "I think this t-t-t-teepee's haunted!"

There was a slight illumination from the glowing ashes of the campfire. All we could make out was a pair of bare feet stumbling around the teepee.

"Hey Pop . . . wake up," I stuttered. "I think there's a ghost in here!"

The groans were replaced by an eerie voice.

"Ids no doast," the voice grunted. "Ma phlucking mouf ids numb!"

The pair of feet started walking toward us. We swallowed hard as the feet got closer and closer. With each step you could hear them flatten down on the dirt floor of the teepee. As the feet got too close for comfort, one of them stepped down on a couple of my sharp arrowheads.

"Aaaargh!" the voice bellowed out in pain. "*Whut da phluck?*"

A pair of hands reached down and picked up my bow and arrows. Whatever it was, it now had my weapon! Beef readied his tomahawk in case it was needed. A bright flash of lightening, seen through the top flap of the teepee, lit up the inside just enough that we could make out the owner of the bare feet. It was a quick glance, but you'd be amazed at what you can see in that instance. The Indian headdress, the disfigured face and my bow and arrow told us all we needed to know. Taking all that into account plus the fact that his underwear sure as hell looked like a loin cloth to us, it's no wonder that we both came to the same *definite* conclusion.

"*Tripping Beaver!*" we screamed. "*He's gonna kill us!*"

"Ah'm nod Frippin' Beafer!" Tripping Beaver said. "Ah'm Da Chieth . . . now knock id off an doe bag to sheep!"

When you're in such an extreme moment of panic, your mind begins to play tricks on you. Mine was no exception. In the flickering illumination that the lightening provided, I saw the specter of Tripping Beaver draw one of my arrows and seat it in the bowstring. The vengeful ghost was going to shoot me in my sleeping bag with my own bow and arrow! Beef must've seen the same thing. He reacted quickly and came to my defense.

"Take that you old ghost!" he shouted as he brought the tomahawk down on Tripping Beaver's foot!

"Al Yi Yi Yi Yi!" Tripping Beaver screamed whilst hopping around the teepee. It sure sounded like the old Chippewa war cry to us.

"Run!" I shouted. Beef and I launched out of our sleeping bags and shot out of the teepee into the pouring rain. Tripping Beaver quickly stumbled after us.

"Det bag here!" Tripping Beaver bellowed. He gave chase as Beef and I scurried into the darkness of the woods. We hid in some bushes that bordered a trail. We could tell where he was by listening for his assorted moans and groans. It appeared that he was circling us! At one point, he came limping by within a few feet of us. He was still clutching my bow and arrow.

"What about The Chief?" Beef asked.

"He's a goner," I answered, "Tripping Beaver already got him! We're on our own now."

"Hey, I got an idea," Beef whispered, "we'll set a trap for ol' Trippin' Beaver!"

He pulled a length of kite string out of his pocket. I jumped over to the other side of the trail, and we tied the string around two trees. The tripwire was strung across the trail, and Tripping Beaver was getting ready to make another pass. I picked up a large stick and held it like a baseball bat, Beef readied his tomahawk and the moans and sloppy footsteps got closer. Time stood still as Tripping Beaver walked the last few yards to our position. Closer... just a few more feet now. Beef and I were in attack position.

SPLAT!

Tripping Beaver lived up to his namesake and stumbled over the kite string, landing face down in the mud. We immediately jumped out of the bushes and attacked. Tripping Beaver bellowed as we whacked him repeatedly with the stick and the tomahawk. The bludgeoning only infuriated Tripping Beaver who slowly rose to his feet with Beef and I still attached and whacking with all our might. The terrible ghost roared out in anger and the mud dripping off of him looked like flesh peeling off his bones! It was hideous! We gave up our attack and retreated back to the bushes. I noticed my bow and arrows lying on the ground and quickly grabbed them before diving into the brush. Tripping Beaver tried to circle around and catch us on the other side. We reversed direction and made a beeline for Mr. Lightfeather's camp.

All we had was the lightening flashes to guide our way through the night. When we got to Mr. Lightfeather's camp, Tripping Beaver was already there. Stalking the grounds in search of fresh blood, no doubt! Mr. Lightfeather heard the commotion and stuck his head out of the tent.

"What's going on?" he said. "Who's out there?"

Tripping Beaver started toward the opening of the tent, moaning and grunting.

"Of all things holy," Mr. Lightfeather gasped. "You better take yourself back to the spirit world, Tripping Beaver. I ain't got no beef with you."

"Ugh blah hookin' pho Deef n' Teeven," Tripping Beaver mumbled.

"I don't understand Chippewa, but I do understand this!" Mr. Lightfeather shouted. He pointed his shotgun barrel out the tent. Tripping Beaver looked horrified and madly waved his hands in air.

"Your magic ain't gonna work on me, demon!" Mr. Lightfeather said. He fired one shot into the air in an attempt to ward off the evil spirit. Tripping Beaver jumped back, but kept waving his hands and, again, started toward Mr. Lightfeather, moaning and grunting...

"The next shot is gonna send you back to hell, Tripping Beaver, unless you turn around right now and go back from where you came!" Mr. Lightfeather warned. He started scurrying around for another shotgun shell. "Where in the hell are my shells?"

Tripping Beaver was still going for Mr. Lightfeather.

"He's gonna get him!" Beef shouted.

"Not if I can help it!" I said. I loaded my bow and brought the arrow back until the kite string hummed. The evil ghost was almost on top of Mr. Lightfeather, waving his arms and grunting fiercely. My hands were shaking as I let the arrow fly...

"*Ayeeeeeeee!*" Tripping Beaver screamed as the arrow struck him in the backside. It was a perfect shot! The arrow left my bow like a laser and hit the gluteus maximus of the intended target... exactly where I aimed it. Too bad the arrow head wasn't sharper, it might've stuck instead of just opening up a nice gash and falling to the ground. At the moment of impact, Tripping Beaver let out the high pitched yelp and began dancing around the campfire in an obvious Chippewa war dance. The Chief would've been proud that I was able to make such a perfect shot. It was too bad that ol' Tripping Beaver got him before he had a chance to see me make that shot. Tripping Beaver danced away into the bushes clutching his right "cheek" and screaming. Soon, it was quiet...

Beef and I congratulated ourselves with high fives while Mr. Lightfeather pulled out a bottle of whiskey, chugged down

THE FISH OF A THOUSAND CASTS

a large portion of it, and retreated to the inside of the tent. Tripping Beaver was defeated.

"*Arrrrrrrrrggggggggghhhhhhh!*" Tripping Beaver roared as he jumped out of the bushes behind us. His eyes were fierce with rage and glowed like embers from a campfire! We screamed and took off running toward the river. The Indian poltergeist was hot on our heels, screaming and yelling. The Chief's new canoe was within distance, our only chance for escape. Beef and I pushed it into the current and dove in, paddling as if our lives depended on it... which, from our perspective, it did. Tripping Beaver started running down the bank after us.

"Teeven, bing bag duh nod ram ganoe!" Tripping Beaver hollered. We paddled faster and soon started to out distance the ghost.

"Teeven! Dumb back!" the ghost hollered. He tripped over a log and landed face down in the water. He looked up and hollered. "Dumb back... Dumb back!"

It was morning when we came across an access site. A couple of fishermen helped us pull the canoe to shore and called the sheriff. We were wrapped in blankets and the sheriff was getting ready to motor up river in search of The Chief's body and to check on the welfare of Mr. Lightfeather. A small boat came around the bend with two people.

The boat got closer and we could make out that one of the people was Mr. Lightfeather. You could spot his pony tail a mile away. The other person looked familiar... it was The Chief. He got away from Tripping Beaver after all, and was alive! It must've been quite a struggle as my father was battered, beaten and bruised. He jumped out of the canoe and started limping after me with his typical angered glare. I guess he was a little upset that we'd abandoned him, but what were we to do? *We thought he was dead...*

Thankfully, the sheriff subdued him before he got to me. Beef and I rode home with my mother, who came to the sheriffs department to claim us. When the whole story was pieced together and everyone, except The Chief, had a good laugh over it, I placed myself under her protection. The Chief *was not* going to let this little misunderstanding go by without retribution!

Thank God, my mom was there to protect me...

A Little Fresh Air

I had just settled down in front of my television to enjoy a Sunday afternoon watching our beloved grid iron gladiators, the Detroit Lions. A tall cool glass of grape soda and piping hot frozen pizza joined me in my laziness. The game was just getting started when my phone rang.

"Hello?" I answered, annoyed that my seclusion and laziness were being interrupted.

"What are you doing?" The Buckmaster asked.

"Its Sunday... you know what I'm doing!" I said.

"Uh huh... they're going to lose," The Buckmaster continued, "me and Smiley are going out to the range to sight in our shot guns... wanna come along?"

"Not really... I'm not in the mood to go out there" I answered.

"You need a little fresh air?" he said. "Great, I'll be over in a few minutes!"

"No! I said I wasn't in the mood to go there," I clarified, "I didn't say anything about fresh air..."

"You're right... it is a nice day for some fresh air!" The

Buckmaster exclaimed. "See ya in a few!"

"*I didn't say* . . ." The Buckmaster hung up before I could finish.

Drat! No matter how scarce I make myself on Sunday afternoons someone always finds a way to sabotage my football viewing plans. It was a nice day though and a severe cold front was on its way; perhaps getting out and enjoying a little fresh air before the front hit wouldn't be so bad after all.

I quickly gulped down my pizza and threw on my hiking boots and insulated flannel. The Buckmaster pulled up in his small rust bucket pickup, complete with its trademark genuine deer antler hood ornament, shortly thereafter. Allow me to add that the hood ornament was a REAL antler, crudely screwed into the hood of the truck. This decrepit old rust bucket was known throughout the county as "The Buck-Mobile". The horn was made to sound like a buck grunt and where some people like to hang a squirrel tail from their antenna, The Buckmaster had . . . you guessed it . . . a deer tail flailing about on his!

"The radio work in this thing?" I asked as we rumbled down the road.

"Only gets AM," The Buckmaster replied.

"Perfect . . . the game is only on AM anyway!" I said. We pulled up at Smiley's house and he crammed into the front seat of the pickup.

"Weird seeing you," Smiley said to me, "usually you don't leave the house on Sunday."

"I needed a little fresh air," I answered.

"You say you got on your best underwear?" The Buckmaster queried.

"What?" I answered.

"Huh?" Smiley added. "He didn't say anything about underwear?"

"Yeah . . . it is a nice day for some fresh air!" The Buckmaster said.

THE FISH OF A THOUSAND CASTS

"His allergies must be acting up," Smiley chuckled. Smiley always chuckles. "His ears are all stuffed up again!"

"Huh?" The Buckmaster grunted.

"NOTHING!" I yelled.

"No need to yell," The Buckmaster said. "I ain't deaf..."

I grew tired of the conversation and turned up the volume on the radio. Even though the Lions were losing badly, it was still better than trying to argue with a man that couldn't hear! It wasn't long before we pulled up to Beef's grandma's house. Beef rambled out with shotgun in tow.

"How are we all supposed to fit in here?" he asked.

"Just pile in!" The Buckmaster said.

"There is no way that all of us are going to fit in here!" I said. "I'll just get in the back."

Beef stuffed himself into the front seat and I sprawled out in the back of the little pick up. We started rumbling down the road again when I noticed that I wasn't alone in the bed of the truck.

"How long has this thing been back here?" I tried to shout through the rear window. I was accompanied by a rather ugly and crudely tanned deer hide. It was grotesque, falling apart and stunk to high heaven. All I wanted to do was curl up on my couch and watch a crummy football game. The stench I was inhaling was not at all what I considered "fresh air"!

"You like that?" The Buckmaster yelled. " I tanned that myself!"

"I never would've guessed!" I answered with a sarcastic tone.

I tried to settle comfortably in a corner of the truck bed. It was cold back there and the rotting deer hide would occasionally attempt to snuggle up next to me. Thankfully, there was an old broomstick handy... which I used to keep the carcass at bay.

Our next stop was at a gas station. The Buckmaster

recognized one of the vehicles at the pump and decided that now was a good time to shoot the bull. The vehicle belonged to an individual named Grubby Gary. Grubby Gary was pretty well known in Hillsdale County. His disdain for personal hygiene and cleanliness in general made for a notoriety that was hard to forget. He and The Buckmaster were very good friends of course. Grubby's truck was filled to the brim with a load of firewood. As we waited for him to come out of the gas station, several customers filtered out holding their noses. Some came out and dropped to their knees in a feeble attempt to draw in some fresh air. Grubby Gary finally emerged as the clerk passed out behind the counter. One brave soul rushed in and frantically dialed 911.

Grubby Gary was a tall, lanky individual whose appearance was ... well, to put it nicely ... rough. In his tattered stocking cap, mud covered goulashes, and flannel jacket that looked like it'd been through fires, floods and numerous bloody road kill butcherings, Grubby Gary made the simple folk look like debutantes! He was ravenously attacking a Slim Jim when he came up to the buck mobile.

"You guys are just in time," Grubby Gary said while spraying particles of Slim Jim everywhere. "I could use a little help unloading this wood!"

"I thought we were going to sight in our guns." Beef whispered to The Buckmaster.

"Aw, this won't take long," The Buckmaster said. "We can help him out ... besides, his house is on the way to the gun range."

I didn't like the idea at all. The cold front and associated ice storm was moving in from the west. I wanted to get this over with and get back to watching football. I was unable to protest, however, as the combination of the retched deer hide and Grubby Gary's body odor had me lightheaded and nauseous. I moaned weakly and The Buckmaster took that as a gesture of my approval.

THE FISH OF A THOUSAND CASTS

"Uh... he doesn't look so good," Smiley said.

"He'll be alright," The Buckmaster advised. "He's been in the house too much. His body don't know how to react to a little fresh air!"

"Wait till he gets a dose of some good hard work!" Grubby Gary said. "Hell, we'll probably have to give him mouth to mouth!" He broke into a huge grin that revealed a set of teeth that hadn't seen a toothbrush in years. Lord only knows how bad his breath was... if you could get past the body order, that is. The thought of Grubby Gary administering CPR to *anyone* made me faint.

When I awoke, we were back on the road. A slight mist of freezing rain had begun to fall and I was wrapped up nicely in a furry blanket. A powerful stench filled my nostrils and as my head cleared I realized where it was coming from. My furry warm blanket was that disgusting deer hide! I jumped up, let out a high pitched wail and kicked the rotting atrocity off of me. The hide tried to leap back onto me but after a brief panic-stricken battle, I was able to subdue it with the broomstick. Apparently, at the same time I jumped up to vanquish the rotting hide, the Lions scored a touchdown. The occupants in the cab, who were still listening to the game on the radio, mistook my jumping about as a sign of celebration.

"He takes those football games way too seriously," The Buckmaster said as he witnessed my plight unfold in his rear view mirror.

"Yeah, he does need to get out of the house more..." Smiley chuckled.

The rest of the ride to Grubby Gary's house consisted of me huddled in the corner of the truck bed getting pelted by pebbles of freezing rain. I clutched the broomstick like a sword and waited for further signs of life from the mangy hide.

I was the first one out of the truck when we arrived and welcomed the opportunity to unload the firewood. I needed the strenuous activity to warm my chattering body.

"I think the fresh air finally kicked in!" The Buckmaster observed. "Notice how motivated he is now?"

Beef, Smiley and I, began the task of unloading the wood. Grubby Gary and The Buckmaster sat down on a log and contributed by shouting directions as to where to pile the wood. When the wind was blowing the right way, Grubby Gary's stench was noticeable even through the freezing rain. When the wind would shift, a strange new odor would filter by. It wasn't Grubby Gary and it wasn't the rank deer hide. I looked around trying to detect the source of this new scent. There was a puddle of some strange ooze bubbling from the ground a few yards behind us. It wasn't oil but it was dark colored and steaming. The puddle was percolating like a fresh pot of coffee. Blub, blub, blub . . .

"Hey Gary?" I said. "When was the last time you had your septic tank emptied?"

"Never have!" he answered. "What's the point? It's just going to get filled up again!"

"Good point!" The Buckmaster commented. "Quit worrying about the septic tank and hurry up with that wood! I wanna get to the range while it's still daylight!"

Beef and I paused long enough to glare at the two slave drivers. We both mumbled the same expletive and continued unloading the wood. Even Smiley was getting irritated and nothing ever gets him down.

"This is not what I had in mind for a Sunday afternoon," he mumbled. His trademark grin was gone. I was beyond irritated. Septic tanks, rotting deer hides and Grubby Gary was not my idea of "a little fresh air". We continued on in our servitude . . .

Beef was the first to mutiny. He propped up a large log and sat down with his arms crossed.

"You ain't gonna get that wood unloaded by sittin' on your duff!" Grubby Gary hollered.

"Your right!" Beef shot back. "It's your wood . . . you

THE FISH OF A THOUSAND CASTS

unload it!"

"You gonna let your nephew talk to me like that?" Grubby Gary said to The Buckmaster. "Somebody ought to smack him upside his ears!"

"What do you mean you ain't seen me in years," The Buckmaster turned and answered. He looked confused, "I helped you put that woodstove in last week!"

"Years? *EARS!*" Grubby Gary shouted. "Ain't *your* damn ears workin'?"

"Huh?" The Buckmaster grunted.

"Oh for cryin' out loud!" I sighed. I heaved a large log from the back of the truck and dropped it on the ground. The middle of the log was somewhat hollow and a gray colored object rolled out of the hollow spot. The five of us stared at the object for a moment. We all realized what it was, looked at each other, and finally a proclamation was made.

"*Run like hell!*" Grubby Gary bellowed.

You know...bees usually go into a state of hibernation at that time of year. If by chance they are active in this cold weather, they are vicious and ornery. Apparently, as our luck would have it, the old log offered sufficient thermal refuge to keep them in an active state. The gray object vibrated with a loud buzzing sound as a cloud of angry honeybees filed out in search of vengeance. Everyone scattered as the mighty cloud rose slowly into the air. I was paralyzed with fear. The cloud hovered for a bit looking for a target. Eventually, one of the bees shouted, "There's one!" and pointed at me. I took off running as the cloud surrounded me.

The first sting was quite painful. The second one was not as bad. By the third and beyond, there was too much overall pain to just pinpoint it to one area of my body. I flailed about, kicked, screamed and sprinted at full speed to nowhere in particular. In a brief moment of clarity, I spotted salvation! I accelerated to a mind numbing speed, hurdled a huge stump and dove headfirst into the ice-cold safety of Grubby Gary's duck pond!

When I poked my head up from under the surface, the bees were gone. A trio of white ducks meandered over to say hello to the new visitor. One showed its affection by quacking loudly and chomping down on my ear. I didn't flinch. The ducks escorted me onto the bank of the pond by playfully pecking at my ankles and shoestrings. My mind was filled with thoughts of murder and mayhem as I trudged toward the buck mobile. I envisioned ripping my telephone out of the wall and then wrapping the cord tightly around the Buckmasters neck. Fresh air my . . . well, under the circumstances you can sympathize with my choice of coarse language here. Next, I would attack Beef and Smiley with the broomstick. Smiley for his incessant chuckling and Beef because . . . he's Beef. Enough said. Grubby Gary and his damn firewood would get the grand finale. I was going to take his . . . suddenly it hit me! I was walking, but I wasn't moving! *What the . . . ?*

I looked down and realized that I was sunk up to my knees in some sort of mud pit. The first blast of noxious fumes and the bubbling ooze around me confirmed my worst fears. *It wasn't a mud pit!*

"Would someone please help me out of this sewage?" I calmly asked. *"Before I freakin' kill somebody!!!"*

No one laughed. Beef and Smiley used the broomstick to help pull me out of the stench bog. I stepped out amidst two loud slurps. Minus my hiking boots of course! It didn't really matter that much, as my body was already soaked and numb from the little jump in the pond.

"Can we go get the guns sighted in now?" Beef asked. "It's starting to get a little chilly out here!"

Under normal circumstances, I would've beaten Beef soundly with the broomstick. But my waterlogged clothes were starting to freeze. The stench of the sewage residue did not subside as my pants glazed over and the freezing rain clung to me like a sheet of cellophane. I simply opened the door of the truck and started to get in.

"Oh no you don't!" The Buckmaster yelled. "You're not getting my truck all wet and stinky, get in the back!"

I curled my frozen body into a corner of the truck bed and we made our way toward the gun range. It was going to be quite a while before I was back on my couch, watching football. As I shivered, soaking wet, in the back of the truck, the rancid deer hide slowly crept toward my exposed feet. I didn't fight back. Before I knew it, it was covering me and I welcomed the warmth that the rotting chunk of fur provided. I think it liked the attention. As luck would have it, my exposure to the fresh air had my nose so stuffy that I was spared the stench of the hide and the wretched ooze that clung to my jeans. My ears were pretty stuffed up as well.

"You're gonna have to wash out the back of my truck when we get back!" The Buckmaster hollered from the driver seat.

"*Huh?*" I shouted back.

Beef and the Big Buck

Ah... autumn. If there is a better time of year to be alive, I haven't found it. The peace and serenity of the woods and rivers as they come alive with activity is second to none. The Salmon and Steelhead return to the rivers to tangle with avid anglers, the leaves turn colors in brilliant fashion and football season starts. Autumn is my favorite season.

It's also the time of year when a number of hunting activities begin. People in my part of the state revere this time of year. Deer hunting is the climax of the hunting season and is looked at in the same respect as a national holiday.

Despite my failed experiences at deer hunting, I've still been a casual observer of this fall rite of passage. Many of my compatriots are regular participants in the sport and I root for them every year. Wally is an avid hunter and never comes home empty handed. Whether he's deer hunting, goose hunting, you name it, he always puts food on the table. Same thing with The Buckmaster, his exploits are well known throughout Hillsdale county and people call him out of the

THE FISH OF A THOUSAND CASTS

blue to get advice and pointers on bagging that prized buck. What I can't understand is the perseverance of my closest friend, Beef.

Beef has been hunting since he was of legal age. His uncle is The Buckmaster and he's had his choice of prime hunting spots year in and year out. He's never shot a deer. In fact, he's never even taken a shot at a deer. Ten years and counting... the big zero looms large. As everyone is telling tales about the buck they shot or the monster that ducked their gunfire, Beef is gnashing his teeth and attempting to contain his envy. In Hillsdale he's known as "buck-less Beef".

But he never gives up. As November 15 approaches every autumn, Beef is sighting in his shotgun and building his blind, ever optimistic that this is the year. The season passes and Beef is left to ponder all the what ifs...

"Did you see anything," I'll ask.

"Nope... I'm going to try a different spot tomorrow," is Beef's usual answer.

Therein lies the problem. Beef has no patience. He moves around, he sleeps and he snores. Even I know that you have to remain still when hunting!

Once upon a time, he came close. Oh! How close it was. I was there to verify the events that surrounded his near success as I still partake in the sport occasionally. This is how it happened...

As November 15th approached this particular year, Beef seemed more intense in his preparations for the upcoming hunt. You could tell that the stress of being known as "buckless Beef" was starting to get to him.

He covered the area he was going to hunt with sugar beets, apples, carrots and anything he could get his hands on that a deer would be attracted to. If he could've found an actual doe in heat to chain to his area, he'd have done it... that's how desperate he was to lure a buck into his shooting lane!

As a casual observer, mind you, it was quite amusing to witness his newfound intensity for success. I myself wasn't all that concerned with bagging a deer; my only mission was to seek a hunting blind that *wasn't* located under an acorn tree. My previous hunting experience gave me the knowledge that acorn trees and squirrels are not conducive to a peaceful hunt. Hell, for all I knew, the demon squirrel who terrorized me the year before could still be lurking in trees since I failed to exterminate him in a bitter fit of rage! My blind was situated in an area completely void of any trees.

The Buckmaster had spent most of the summer scouting his area and his blind was installed months prior. His guns were sighted in and all he had to do was wait for the opener. Even he was amazed at Beef's passion.

"It's about time the boy started listening to me," stated The Buckmaster. " Do you know how embarrassing it is to have a blood relative of mine be such a failure at hunting?"

"I listened to you and where did it get me?" I answered. "I got tortured by a demented rodent."

"Hunting is about concentration, you have to block out everything around you and concentrate on the kill." said The Buckmaster in a Yoda like manner.

"I'd like to see you keep your concentration when you're getting pelted with acorns for hours on end!" I retaliated.

"The spirit of the wild is not with you," he said, "and you will never be a hunter until you listen for its call."

The Buckmaster was starting to get creepy. I simply nodded and tried to carry on with what I was doing. Almost everyone in Hillsdale County starts to get a little weird at that time of the year; deer hunting consumes their every thought . . .

Beef's daily ritual was to check his hunting area for signs of deer. He'd walk the area looking for tracks and would check his bait piles to see if anything had been eaten. Three days before the opener, Beef was amazed at what he discovered.

THE FISH OF A THOUSAND CASTS

There was a massive scrape on a tree near his blind and one of the bait piles was nearly gone. A set of very large deer tracks covered the area. The size of the scrape indicated that a set of very large antlers had damaged the bark of the tree. Clearly, the buck of Beef's dreams had staked a claim of the area. Beef replenished the bait pile and didn't sleep much after that. He rambled incessantly about the monster buck that was stalking his blind. The day before the opener, Beef added the coup de grace . . . a large dose of doe in heat scent.

"This will absolutely drive him crazy!" Beef stated. He was a man on a mission. Why else would he spend $38 on a bottle of scent? The man was usually a cheapskate.

Beef and I decided to stay at the Buckmaster's house that evening. We figured it would be easier if all three of us were in the same location come morning. Less hassle rounding everyone up.

The Buckmaster spent the evening meditating in his chair. He felt that his mind had to be completely at ease in order to hear the spirit of the wild the next morning. This is the same man who never speaks of the mighty spirit until a week before hunting season! I had to draw the line when he started chanting like a Mongolian monk.

"Ohmmmmm, Ohmmmmm"

"What are you doing?" I asked.

"Preparing myself for the hunt," The Buckmaster answered. "Your mind must be free to hear the spirit of the wild."

"You're in the living room," I said. "Irritating me with your Gregorian chants isn't going to summon the spirit. Who are you, Fred Bear?"

"You got something against Fred?" The Buckmaster asked.

"No, I have nothing against Mr. Bear . . . he was a woodsman through and through, you on the other hand haven't seen a forest since last year." I quickly shot back.

"I believe in the spirit of the wild," Beef joined in. "I can feel it when I'm hunting... I can feel it moving through me."

"That's just gas," I said, "either that or you're still drunk from the night before!"

I believe in the spirit of the wild, don't get me wrong, but I sense it's presence in other ways; like the wind blowing through the trees or the reflection on a stream at day break. It's omnipresent and powerful but it isn't going to guide a bullet into the chest of a mighty buck. That requires skill and good marksmanship, Beef possesses neither. That's why he's "buck-less Beef". Annoying chants aren't going to summon the spirit either...

The amazing thing about opening day eve was Beef's reluctance to partake of his usual carousing. In years past, he would seek out the spirit of the wild by enjoying the company of a young woman and a case of adult beverages. Tonight he didn't want either one.

"I need to be rested when that big buck comes out," he said. "I can't be napping like I usually am."

Whoa! This definitely was a changed man!

The alarm clock went off at 4:30am. Beef was the first one out of bed and had the coffee ready when I reluctantly stumbled into the kitchen. The Buckmaster was close behind.

"Someone please explain to me why fishing and hunting always have to involve getting up early," I mumbled.

"Because the spirit demands it," The Buckmaster mumbled back. Beef was wide awake and rushing us to drink our coffee. He wanted to get into his blind as soon as possible. You never know when that buck is going to wander through...

A short time later, we were walking down the dark trail towards our hunting area. The county roads were alive with traffic as hunters made there way towards the zillions of acres of cornfields that typically host Hillsdale county hunting activities.

The Buckmaster crawled into his blind, which overlooked a fencerow, and settled into a Zen like trance. Beef and I continued down the trail until we got to his blind.

"I'll just dump another dose of this doe in heat scent and that buck will come running!" Beef stated. He struggled with the cap on his bottle of scent. He grimaced as he attempted to unscrew the lid.

"What's wrong?" I asked.

"Can't get the lid off this stuff," he grunted.

"Bang it on that log over there," I suggested. Beef thumped the lid on the edge of the log a few times. Finally, he wedged the bottle between his legs and put all of his muscle into prying the lid off. The lid broke free but the force of the momentum caused the bottle to fly out from between his legs. A huge amount of liquid splashed out and landed on the front of Beef's carharts. He cursed a couple of times and dumped the remaining fluid on the ground near his bait piles.

"I'll see ya when I shoot that buck!" he said as he wandered toward his blind, the heavy scent of doe in heat trailing him. I continued down the trail and hunkered in my tree-less blind. I had a clear view of Beef's hunting area to my right and occasionally would glance over there to check his progress. Much to my surprise, he was wide-awake and sitting motionless like a statue. For all his perseverance I sincerely hoped that his record of futility would end today . . .

As the sun rose and cast it's warm illumination over the land, the sound of gunshots filled the morning air. Two loud and echoing shots that emanated from the Buckmaster's blind signaled the fall of a six point buck and another triumph for the master. The spirit of the wild rewarded him very early that morning. I wasn't too concerned with shooting a deer, I was happy for his success and really just enjoyed being outdoors on such a fine morning. A flock of wild turkeys emerged from the bushes in front of me and milled about in front of my blind pecking at the dirt for their morning meal. The sound of mourning doves provided a pleasing soundtrack to the display set before me.

I heard a snap of a twig behind me and the mourning doves ceased their cooing. The turkey's raised their heads and glanced in the direction of the sound. Without warning, the turkey's scrambled back into the brush. I slowly turned to see what was up and caught site of the most regal buck I'd ever laid eyes on.

The majestic creature emerged from the trees and started toward Beef's blind. The beast was huge and sported 12 points on its mighty rack. Beef was wide eyed with disbelief as the monster sauntered toward his blind.

When I say sauntered that's not a stretch of the imagination. This buck was cool. He inhaled the scent of a doe in heat and smoothly maneuvered towards its source with one thing in mind. Mr. Buck was looking to score.

The beast sniffed the air several times and strutted toward the blind in a manner similar to someone entering the playboy mansion. He had that John Travolta-Saturday Night Fever Strut down pat and the only thing missing was a fur covered pimp hat and dark sunglasses! Hell, I thought the creature was going to light a cigarette at any moment. Beef was taken aback by the bucks immense size and demeanor and was clearly nervous. He had no idea that his futility was going to be broken by such a huge creature!

The buck, meanwhile, started scraping the ground around the bait pile with his mighty antlers. He stomped his feet a couple of times before raising his head. He sniffed the air again in an attempt to locate the doe in heat and slowly turned his head toward Beef's blind. The buck's eyes caught Beef's eyes and the animal let out a smooth grunt that sounded eerily similar to Barry White. I swear I heard the romantic sounds of Luther Vandross music fill the air as Mr. Buck gave Beef a wink and began strutting toward the blind. When a buck that

THE FISH OF A THOUSAND CASTS

big is in the rut they're oblivious to everything around them. They have one thing and only one thing on their mind. Beef quickly raised his shotgun and aimed at the beast as it slid ever closer to the blind. The buck let out another Barry White like grunt as Beef pulled the trigger on the gun.

CLICK! CLICK! CLICK!

The idiot Beef, in all his preparation, had forgotten to load his shotgun! In an act that could have easily come from that show *"When Animals Attack"*, the buck jumped into the blind with Beef. Clearly Mr. Buck was eager to consummate their newfound relationship.

Beef threw his shotgun at the love struck buck and started running like a madman across the field. The buck wasn't about to let his doe in heat get away and chased after him.

Mr. Buck was gaining on Beef and at one point attempted to jump on Beef's back. Beef scrambled up the nearest tree he could find and clawed his way to a safe distance off the ground. I was simply awestruck at the whole spectacle and could only watch with mouth wide open. The Buckmaster wandered down the trail to look for Beef and I. When he focused in on the activities afoot, *his* mouth dropped to the ground. The buck circled the tree, grunting, and made several attempts to shake Beef off the branch he was clinging to.

"Shoot it! Shoot it!" Beef screamed.

"I can't!" shouted the Buckmaster. "I already filled my tag!"

"Steve! Get over here and shoot this thing!"

I jumped up from my blind and ran toward the tree. I stood beside the Buckmaster and aimed my weapon at the monster buck's chest.

"Dear God! Shoot it!" Beef pleaded. The Buck was digging his hooves into the bark of the tree and was actually trying to climb the damn thing! I was laughing so hard that I couldn't hold the gun straight. The Buck had almost figured out how to get to Beef.

"What are you waiting for!" Beef screamed. "Pull the trigger!"

I couldn't do it. All that creature wanted was a little companionship and I certainly didn't want someone shooting me while I was trying to get lucky... although a few irate fathers had attempted it in the past! I pointed the gun in the air and rattled off three quick shots. The sound of the thunderous release caused the buck to snap from his erotic trance and realize what he'd gotten himself into. He took one look at us and sprinted back into the woods, never to be seen again.

"Why didn't you shoot it?" asked the Buckmaster.

"You want someone to shoot you the next time your in bed with your wife?" I said.

"Well... yeah! I hope someone would put me out of misery!" he answered.

"When the day comes for me to shoot a buck, it's not going to be while he's trying to score!" I said. "Jeez, have a heart!"

"*I ain't no deer's wife!*" Beef shouted from his branch.

It took quite a bit of coaxing to get Beef out of the tree. Once he finally came down, he immediately sprinted toward the safety of the truck. As he jumped in, he locked the doors behind him. We drove back home with the Buckmaster's deer in the back of the pick up. The Buckmaster couldn't stop laughing the entire way.

"I'll say this," he said between chuckles, "that scent you bought really works!"

"Nobody says a word about any of this... got it?" Beef threatened. "And you, Mr. outdoor writer, I don't wanna see any damn articles about this either!"

Ok, I kept my word. I didn't write any *articles* about this. What I wrote here is a *humorous short story*... there's a huge difference you know! Besides, it's not like Beef will ever read this. He'll never know...

One of Those Days

There's a certain camaraderie that exists amongst sportsmen. When one hunter meets another in the woods or an angler encounters a fellow fisherman on the river, a conversation will usually be struck up.

"How'd ya do today?" is the most common question asked when fellow outdoorsmen run into each other.

"Eh, not so good . . . it's been one of *those* days!" will be the usual answer.

That's the common thread that ties all individuals who participate in outdoor activities together. Whether you're a hunter or a fisherman, everyone (and I mean everyone) has "one of those days".

Professional anglers have "one of those days", as do avid hunters like The Buckmaster. "One of those days" is the type of day where everything that can go wrong . . . does.

A bad day will usually begin when an outdoorsman wakes up in the morning . . . an hour after first hitting the snooze alarm and well past the prime, morning, hunting and fishing times. Once the individual is up and around, the next indication of a bad day will be the weather. Weather in Michigan is predicated on the odds that someone is going to be hunting or fishing. Due to the likelihood that someone *is* going to be doing either or, the weather conditions will appropriately fall into the following: rain, snow, cold, and wind or any combination of the four. Since we know that any of those conditions will be present, it's kind of like playing "Jeopardy" when you get up in the morning.

"I'll take rain and wind for $200, Alex!"

Of course, no bad day is complete without forgetting something. Forgetting your coffee thermos is a pretty good way to start a bad day. If you're a smoker, drop the only lighter you have in the water . . . when your miles away from your vehicle! Nothing adds to a bad day like having a full pack of cigarettes with no way in God's creation to light them. It's the little things like that that let a bad day get out of hand. The big things are the exclamation point of the whole affair.

To give you a prime example of "one of those days", allow me to venture back in time a few years and share with you a day where everything went wrong . . .

Back in the days when I owned a '78 Chevy extended van (otherwise known as the "sex mobile") Wally, Beef, and I traveled to the Paw Paw River to tangle with some Chinook Salmon that had migrated in from the St. Joseph River. We left Hillsdale at three o' clock in the morning. The trek to the river usually took us two hours and leaving at three a.m. would put us there early enough to claim some choice pools. None of us had been to bed yet so we took turns driving. Just as we were about to arrive, a heavy down pour erupted (Imagine that!). We pulled into the parking area, which was empty, about 4:45 a.m. and decided to wait for the rain to settle down. A few bursts of lightening confirmed that our decision to wait was a wise one.

I'd slept most of the way over (not an easy thing to do when you're driving) so I told Wally and Beef to catch a few

THE FISH OF A THOUSAND CASTS

Z's while I read my paper and monitored the weather conditions. They crashed out in the back of the van while I read my sports page. The occasional rumble of thunder and the steady cadence of rain pattering on the roof of the van was mesmerizing...

It was daylight when I was jolted suddenly from a deep sleep.

The rain had subsided to a light drizzle and the parking lot was filled up considerably. Wally opened his eyes, saw that it was light out, and jumped up from his sleeping bag.

"I thought you were watching the weather!" he said.

"I was!" I answered, folding up the crumpled remains of my sports page. "I must've dozed off."

Wally shook Beef in an attempt to wake him up.

"Wake up!" he shouted. "We need to get down to the river!"

"I never kissed your daughter sir," Beef mumbled while rolling over, "it just looked that way."

Beef was finally raised from the dead and since most of the prime spots near the parking lot were already taken we had to resort to plan "B".

Plan "B" was to drive down to a more secluded spot that was near some gravel runs that attracted a few Salmon. We puttered down a muddy two-track until we reached the edge of a steep hill. The hill over-looked the river and we'd have to hike down to get to the river. The rain was still falling of course. We donned our waders, assembled our fishing gear, and looked for a way to get down the hill.

"There's a deer trail over there we can navigate down," Wally said.

"We're not deer," stated Beef, "we don't have hooves."

There was no alternative, so we started down the narrow deer path. The rain had made the trail slippery and with each step we took it felt as if our feet were going to come out from under us. We tiptoed a few feet at a time and used the trees around us for support. I was leading the way with Wally and Beef close behind. I felt myself starting to slip so I grabbed a hold of the nearest thing I could find: Wally's arm. Wally and I both started to slip so we tried to grab onto a tree that was just behind us. I was attached to Wally's arm, Wally grabbed a tree branch, and in the process his rod smacked Beef in the side of the head. The "whack" to the side of Beef's head was relatively painless but it was just enough to assist him in losing his balance. Beef slid by Wally and I before losing complete control of his feet. He tumbled a few times before landing at the water's edge with a loud "thump!" He sat there, seething, as Wally and I finished our treacherous journey down unscathed.

"Here," I said, "you dropped your rod on the way down."

Beef's response made it quite clear that he was unappreciative of my rod retrieval efforts. Jeez! the nerve of some people. You try to do something nice and they hurl insults at you!

Ok, it was still raining, we fell asleep and missed out on the easily accessible fishing spots, and Beef tumbled down a muddy slope. As you can see, it was already turning out to be "one of those days." To add to things, I left my cigarettes and coffee thermos in the van. I was already starting to get irritated from nicotine and caffeine withdrawal.

Wally spotted a few Salmon darting around a gravel bed upstream and decided to try that spot first. Beef and I started walking downstream in search of another group of Salmon. After walking a few yards we found a nice batch of fish holding on the edge of a tailout. From the side of the river we were on, the tailout was unfishable. A large tree branch hung over the bank of the river making it impossible to cast. In order to try for those fish, we'd have to cross the river and cast from the other side. We didn't want to spook the fish by crossing there so we backtracked upstream a little ways and attempted to cross in a harmless looking spot.

THE FISH OF A THOUSAND CASTS

Beef started out first and announced that the current was stronger than it looked. He waddled across while fighting the current (the water was past his waist) and, eventually got to the other side. I'm pretty cocky when it comes to crossing rivers and have a feeling of invincibility. After watching Beef make it across, I determined that navigating the current would be no problem. With reckless abandon I hopped into the river and began plodding across.

I made it a few feet before a nasty log decided to make my day interesting. The log, which had been lying dormant on the river bottom for eons, suddenly came to life and lashed out at my feet. At that point, I flawlessly executed a "head first plunge". The plunge was perfect in form and technique. To finish the routine, I concluded the presentation by "dog paddling" the rest of the way across the river. Beef was beside himself with fits of laughter. I quickly thought of a nonchalant saying to avoid looking stupid.

"I figured I wouldn't wait for the rain to soak me," I said.

"What's that splashing going on down there?" Wally hollered. "Somebody got a fish on or did "Splash" fall in again?"

"Splash" is one of my *many* nicknames.

Now that I was thoroughly soaked, Beef and I made our way down to the tailout and got ready to fish. It was a perfect spot that was snag free and a dozen feisty Chinook were scattered about on the gravel. The fish were not spooked from the activities around them as they were solely focused on their fatal spawning routine. Beef and I were rigging our rods up when we heard the sounds of a fish leaping frantically.

"Fish on!" Wally hollered. "Coming down!"

Wally was engaged in a fierce battle with a bulldog of a Salmon. The fish leaped out of the water several times and made numerous runs downstream in an attempt to free the hook from his bony jaw. Wally saw that the fish was running towards our tailout and being the courteous type that he is applied heavy pressure to the rod in an effort to stop the Salmon's momentum.

"Put the brakes on that pig!" I yelled.

"Don't spook our fish!" Beef hollered.

"Don't worry," answered Wally. "I'm just going to put a little pressure on him and turn him just like..."

SNAP!

The fish shot out of the water in a spectacular jump and Wally's rod snapped into three pieces. The Chinook, free of the hook, swam away while Wally stood motionless and stared at the shattered remains of his custom-built drift rod. Not known as one with a foul mouth, Wally unleashed the most extreme vernacular he could think of.

"PHOOEY!"

He stormed out of the river and began clawing his way up the muddy hill so he could retrieve his spare rod from the back of the van. For every positive step he made, he'd slide backward two steps. It was going to be awhile before he got to the top. Beef and I focused on the Salmon milling about in front of us.

To make the weather conditions worse, a nice strong wind had recently come up making casting a little more difficult. I stripped a few feet of line off my fly reel and flipped a well-tied "Hutchins Hairball" toward the pod of Salmon. The tie didn't hit the water. In fact, the wind got a hold of my offering when it was in mid air and carried it into the tree branch on the other side of the river. I tried a few times to pull it off the branch to no avail so I broke it off and tied on a new rig.

Again, I stripped some line off the reel and flipped the rig toward the Salmon. Again, the wind carried the offering into the tree branch.

"You might want to consider having that branch mounted," Beef said sarcastically. "It's pretty big..."

Now I was mad. Not only was it raining buckets and I was soaked from head to toe, but I couldn't even get a cast

THE FISH OF A THOUSAND CASTS

into the river. My friend's sarcasm didn't help matters either. Beef flipped his offering perfectly into the path of the waiting Salmon.

"No problem what so ever," he mocked. His tie drifted past the Salmon and a surly male fish chomped down on it.

"There we go!" Beef said. "Just that quick".

The fish darted around the proximity of the tailout bound and determined to free himself of the hook. Beef applied pressure to the rod and the fish decided to make a break for it down stream. The reel screamed as the fish peeled off line like a Marlin off the Florida Keys. Beef dug his heels into the river bottom and used every ounce of arm strength trying to turn the fish back upstream. Feeling the pressure of the rod, the fish had no choice but to leap straight out of the water. As the fish was completely airborne the hook dislodged from his mouth and due to the heavy pressure on the line, the rig shot back in Beef's direction.

THWAP! Beef's sinkers hit him squarely in the forehead, caromed off me, and landed in the bushes directly behind us. Beef gave me a dazed look and fell backwards into the water.

"You might want to duck next time," I told Beef as he crawled onto the riverbank.

We heard a muffled shout and turned in time to watch Wally sliding backwards, on his stomach, down the hill. He had just about made it to the top when his footing gave way and down he went. He made every attempt to scratch and claw himself to a stop but the slide continued until he reached the bottom. He cartwheeled a couple times before landing on his back in the icy cold river.

SPLASH!

Most of the Salmon in our vicinity scattered for cover and disappeared.

"That was nice," I muttered.

This had turned out to be the mother of all bad days and we were left with no choice but to surrender to the fishing gods and call it a day. We struggled our way back up the hill and a mere two hours later flopped our weary and broken bodies at the top. I looked down at the river and saw that the Salmon had come out of hiding... that figures.

Sometime during our journey back up the hill the rain had stopped. We were packing our gear into the van when a burst of sunlight peaked through the cracks in the clouds. The clouds were breaking up quickly and soon after we pulled off of the two track the fishing gods mocked us with clear blue skies.

"Well, where we gonna go tomorrow?" I asked.

"Tomorrow?" Wally said. "Heck, it's turning into a nice day... isn't that other spot we go to just up the road?"

"Yep."

"Let's give it a shot," Wally said, "the day is still young!"

"I hope someone notifies my next of kin..." Beef muttered from the back of the van. Salmon fever is an addictive force. Ignoring the will of the fishing gods, we pulled into the next stop and assembled our equipment. As we made our way toward the river another round of dark clouds appeared on the western horizon. We weren't surprised.

You have to be ready for *anything* when you're having "one of those days"...

Death of a Sportsman

Two fellows are fishing in a boat under a bridge. One looks up and sees a funeral procession starting across the bridge. He stands up, takes off his cap and bows his head. The procession crosses the bridge and the man puts his cap back on, picks up his rod and reel and continues fishing. The other guy says, "That was touching. I didn't know you had it in you."

The first guy responds, "Well, I guess it was the thing to do. After all... I was married to her for 40 years!"
—*Old fisherman's joke ... Author unknown.*

The telephone rang at my place of employment the other day.

"Did you get your invitation yet?" asked my good friend Wally after I answered the phone.

"What invitation?" I asked.

"Smiley's getting married!" he answered.

"Oh... that invitation," I replied, "yeah, I got it... I thought you were talking about something else."

"What else would I be talking about?" he asked.

"I don't know... I thought maybe I was getting invited to something jovial, a celebration perhaps, not something fatal like a wedding," I answered.

Now, allow me to take a moment to apologize for what seems to be a bitter attitude toward marriage. In recent months my own marriage had eroded and the idea of the institution did not sit well with me. Everyone makes mistakes and I'm no exception. You never take someone whose life revolves around the outdoors and pair them up with an individual whose only idea of "wild life" is a night of club hopping. Still, a vow is a vow and despite the fact that my life was definitely changing for the better, I was somewhat angered that my W.I.F.E. and I had drifted apart and separated. At the time of Wally's phone call my mental state viewed marriage as something less than favorable. If my own marriage couldn't be held together, how was I supposed to get exited about someone else's impending nuptials? I suppose I was closer to the dreaded 'D' word than I ever wanted to be... in hindsight though, it was the best thing that ever happened to me!

"Just because you're bitter, doesn't mean that marriage is a bad thing," said Wally, "look at me..."

Wally is happily married, an oxymoron of course, and his wife is actually a decent woman, even though she doesn't like me! I'm not opposed to marriage and my girlfriend, Steph, has forced me to rethink my hesitance in ever entering into it again. But it just seems that once a sportsman gets married, the odds are high that he'll never be seen or heard from again. His guns will gather dust in the gun cabinet and his fishing rods will be sold at the next garage sale as he's miserably trimming the hedges and watering the lawn. Wally falls into that category. His fishing and hunting adventures are now few and far between.

"Smiley wants to run over to the Joe with us to do a little fishing... kinda like a bachelor party I guess," said Wally. The Joe is our nickname for the St. Joseph River. We'd heard that a run of summer Steelhead was in and we planned on heading over there for the weekend.

"Who's going to administer last rites?" I asked.

"I think it will be good for you to get away as well!" he said.

I used to be the kind of sportsman who was always in the outdoors. Sun up to sun down with no time limits and not a care in the world. Along the way I'd meet lots of fellow outdoor enthusiasts who sported wedding bands on their left-hand ring fingers. Each would tell the tale of how they tricked their spouse into letting them go out fishing and hunting or, better yet, would brag of being "the man of the house" and that they didn't have any time limit because the wife "knows who's boss!" More often than not, our conversations ended with the bold woodsman saying: "Holy cow! Look at the time... my wife is going to kill me!" The sportsman would pack up his gear and run, not walk, back to his car...

During those days, I was a bit bold myself and proclaimed that if I ever got married I would still fish and hunt as much as I did now. Usually my statements were met with fits of hysterical laughter from the married guys who overheard me.

"Hey Earl!" they'd say, "did ya hear what he said?"

"Yeah... Oh man, I'm laughing so hard my stomach hurts!"

"Holy Cow, Earl! Look at the time..."

When I got married I realized that I *wasn't* going to fish and hunt as much as I used to. It wasn't my wife saying directly that I couldn't go but I could sense a whole lot of pressure to be home at a certain time. What fun is being in the outdoors if you have to look at your watch all the time? Once she was, thankfully, out of the picture, my fishing activities returned to normal. Coincidence?

Smiley is one of those people who spend a great deal of time outside as well. He loves to fish and hunt and actually has a woman who loves to do both with him. His partner has joined us on numerous excursions and, say what you will, can hold her own in the fishing department. If ever there was a match made in heaven, this is it. I just worry about Smiley though. Women are wonderful chameleons until the wedding ring goes on. In a number of cases once you say, "I do" she's going to snap her head, unleash a maniacal laugh and say "not anymore pal!" Like a trout rolling on the end of your leader, you're hooked! And catch & release isn't one of the options; into the creel you go...

But, enough of my bitter marriage views. At the time of this story, they were skewed and not indicative of how I *truly* feel about the sanctity of matrimony. As always, there is a tale to be told here. Allow me to get back on track...

Wally called me on Tuesday. The outing was scheduled for the upcoming weekend and by Thursday it had turned into an event of epic proportions. At first it was just going to be Wally, Beef, Smiley and myself. As the event grew, we were joined by The Buckmaster and another fellow named Dickens.

Dickens has not been mentioned in previous stories because he rarely comes out of wife induced hiding to join in our adventures. We call him Dickens due to his ability to spawn grand tales out of nothing at all. He is the stereotypical braggart whose accomplishments in the outdoors can never be matched by any mortal man. If he catches *two* Steelhead in one day, the count grows to *twenty-two* by the time he tells the story. Last years spike horn buck that he shot was a twelve pointer that just missed being a Boone and Crockett world record. It's his knack for spinning such grandiose tales that earned him his nickname, which is a reference to Charles

THE FISH OF A THOUSAND CASTS

Dickens. In short, Dickens is what we sportsmen refer to as a "B-S Artist."

When word of the fishing trip/bachelor party spread to The Squirrel, he offered the use of his father's motor home... provided that he was allowed to tag along. We eagerly accepted his offer.

On Friday afternoon our merry party-on-wheels departed. I have to admit that I felt a tweak of my heartstrings as Wally, Dickens and Smiley said goodbye to their better halves. The women wept as if they'd never see their men again; must have been some sort of womanly intuition. What can possibly go wrong when seven men pack into a mobile home for a fishing trip?

Smiley's wedding was scheduled for Sunday at 3:30 in the afternoon. We figured we could keep fishing until Sunday morning at least. The wedding was to be a small affair at the bride's house, attended by a chosen few. Rehearsals and all that stuff weren't required thus allowing Smiley to escape until Sunday. The only words of wisdom his better half gave him were "Be here on time or *everyone* dies!" Coincidentally, the radio blasted out the classic song "Highway To Hell" by AC/DC as the motor home tore out of Smiley's driveway. As I looked out the back window, I noticed Wally's wife make the sign of the cross before falling into a fit of uncontrolled sobbing. Wally himself began to wonder what he'd gotten into; during the two and a half-hour trip to the St. Joe he'd find out...

We were barely on the road when Beef broke out a large cooler containing several assorted adult beverages.

"Anybody want a cold one?" he asked as he popped the top on a frosty can of hops and barley.

"Yeah, give me one," I said, feeling the need to shake off some pent up frustrations.

"What are you guy's doing?!" The Squirrel shrieked, *"THAT'S ILLEGAL!!"*

"Relax, we're in a motor home," Beef said.

"You know my dad's a cop!" The Squirrel informed. "This is open intoxicants in a moving vehicle!"

"We're grown men," I said, "do you really believe he doesn't know that we'd have beer?"

"Yeah," Beef replied, "and there's no way we're gonna get pulled over as slow as *he's* driving"

"*You wanna come up here and drive?!*" The Buckmaster shouted from the driver's seat.

"He can't drive!" said The Squirrel. "He's drinking!"

"I haven't even taken a sip yet!" Beef retorted.

"Alright!" Wally announced, "We're all responsible adults here... put the beer away while we're on the road and then anyone who wants to can get rip roaring drunk once we're safely there... agreed?"

We all agreed. Smiley, as always, just chuckled at the circus-taking place in the back of the motor home. It's not his nature to frown or show displeasure, he simply smiles... *all the time!*

The conversation quickly shifted to the fishing aspect of the trip. Based on the reports we'd heard we were anticipating some decent angling opportunities.

"It should be real good," said Dickens, "me and my uncle pounded 'em last weekend!"

"Who are you kidding, Dickens?" The Buckmaster snorted. "The only thing you did last weekend was mow the lawn!"

"We went over Sunday morning," answered Dickens, "and those fish were just smacking black stone flies like they hadn't eaten for weeks! I got four that were pushing 15 pounds."

"Yeah right!" we all answered in unison.

"We all know as well as you do that your wife wouldn't let you out of the house like this two weekends in a row!" I said.

"I know mine wouldn't," Wally said.

THE FISH OF A THOUSAND CASTS

"I don't know of any wife that would," Beef added, "but then again, I'm not married so who knows?"

"I can get away," The Buckmaster said. "I just fight and argue with my wife all week and when the weekend rolls around she's so sick of me that she literally pushes me out the door!"

We nodded our heads in agreement.

"It's not really like that . . . is it guys?" Smiley asked, sweat starting to form on his forehead. We all just looked at the floor and weakly nodded our heads again.

"Smiley, let me tell ya something," Dickens said. "A woman will let you come and go as you please as long as you . . . handle your business, if you know what I mean, heh heh heh!"

Dickens gave Smiley a playful jab to the ribs.

"Yeah, that's why your wife throws all your clothes in the front yard every time you go fishing . . . huh, Dickens?" Beef laughed.

"And you have to beg her to let you back in!" The Squirrel added.

"Very funny guys . . . very funny," Dickens sulked.

To say the least, the journey to the Joe was a jovial affair. We laughed, waved at people on the side of the road and tried to impart marital wisdom upon poor Smiley. I of course refrained from giving out such advice. If my marriage collapsed after just one year, I certainly can't be giving out blissful advice!

It was dark when we pulled into the parking lot of the Berrien Springs Dam . . . our home for the next two days. Beef unloaded the beer while the rest of us unloaded the necessary fishing equipment. We donned our waders and began the lighting of the lanterns. With the exception of Smiley, we all had those instant light propane jobs that fire up with the click of a button. Smiley had one of the older, fill with gas and pump type lanterns.

He struck a match and placed it under the mantles. An orange ball of flame and black smoke followed.

"The sign over there says no campfires!" Beef said.

Smiley just chuckled and in his "aw shucks" demeanor said: "All I have to do his blow on this and the mantles will start glowing."

He put his face near the bottom of the lantern...

"Watch," he said. "I'll just simply blow on it like this and..."

WOOOOF!!! A huge ball of bright flame went up! Smiley jumped back like a cat in a water puddle and the lantern quickly settled into a soft, white glow.

"Whew!" Smiley said. "That was close!"

"Close?!" The Squirrel started laughing, hysterically. "*Close?* Dude... *you ain't got no freakin' eyebrows!*"

"WHAT?" Smiley shouted, looking at me.

"Nope," I said, "no eyebrows."

"All gone."

Everyone except Smiley broke out in laughter. We could imagine how his wedding pictures would look with him minus eyebrows! That, and the Mr. Clean references, gave us a huge source of jokes at Smiley's expense. He had to endure our good-natured ribbings for the rest of the night.

It was certainly a nice night, that's for sure, but the fishing reports we'd heard were slightly off target. In short, we didn't catch anything that first night. There was one exciting moment when Dickens hooked into a rather large fish and announced that he had a Steelhead on. We all rushed over to watch him battle it and after awhile, I noticed that his rod wasn't shaking like it does when a steelie is fighting.

"Man, that isn't a steelie," I said, "you've got a Carp!"

"Oh listen to you, Mr. Outdoor Writer," Dickens replied, "just cause you write for some outdoor magazines doesn't mean you're a fish expert!"

"No... but I know when someone's hooked into a Carp."

THE FISH OF A THOUSAND CASTS

A few minutes later we stood at the shoreline and admired the huge, bronze colored Carp as it struggled in the landing net. It was really quite a beauty!

"Don't even say a word, Hutchins," Dickens sulked.

Most of us, with the exception of Wally, were beginning to feel the effects of the adult beverages and decided to hang it up for the night. We retreated back to the motor home and piled into our sleeping bags. Beef and I were sharing the top bunk above the driver's seat. Everyone else was scattered in various locations throughout the motor home. The Buckmaster began fumbling with the knobs on the television.

"Hey does thing work?" he said.

"Yeah, it works," answered The Squirrel, "it's even got a VCR under the cabinet..."

"Well, well, well," stated the Buckmaster, "good thing I brought *this* along!"

He held up a videocassette and placed it in the VCR. Beef and I couldn't see the TV but once we heard the pounding, erotic disco music—we knew what kind of tape he'd put in! We hooted and hollered at the television as it displayed it's graphic content.

"Look how long that thing is!" I said. "How can he carry it?"

"Man, I've never seen a woman do *that* before!" Beef said.

"Where did you get this?" asked Wally.

"Mail order," answered The Buckmaster. "Saw it on the outdoor channel... its called 'Trophy Fish of North America—A pro's Guide to catching the big one'."

There were plenty of huge fish on that tape... it was awe inspiring! What did you think we were watching, a porno? Get your minds out of the gutter folks... this book is supposed to be good, clean fun...

When we awoke the next day, the first order of business was to locate two things: breakfast and aspirin. We knew the fishing was dead so we weren't in any hurry to rush down to the river. Besides, as much as my head hurt from the evening prior, I wasn't rushing to do anything! Smiley was the last one out of bed and the rest of us were outside when he finally emerged from the motor home.

"Good morning fella's!" he said with a smile.

We grunted in acknowledgement before something about him caught our attention and all eyes focused on his face.

"What's wrong?" he asked. His face was absolutely beet red from his chin to his forehead. Apparently, the flash of heat that singed his eyebrows off also did more damage. Without his eyebrows his face looked like a big shiny tomato!

The Squirrel laughed so hard that he nearly threw up.

"Oh man," Smiley sighed as he looked in the mirror, "how can I have wedding pictures taken when I look like this?"

"Whose gonna notice?" consoled Wally. "No one really pays attention to wedding pictures anyway!"

After breakfast we decided to try the fishing again. It served little except to pass the day away. We finally abandoned all hope of catching Steelhead and began tossing night crawlers for carp and catfish. I nursed my hangover sprawled out in a lawn chair. The rest of the guys were filling Smiley's head with all kinds of horrible marriage tales. After awhile you could see that he was starting to get cold feet.

"Man, you make it sound like I'm dead," he said.

"Oh no," answered The Buckmaster, "you don't die, you just say goodbye to fishing and hunting as you used to know it . . . from this day forward, just think of it in the past tense."

Smiley gulped and his face became an even brighter shade of red . . .

Later in the afternoon a series of thunderstorms forced us to restrict our activities to inside the motor home. Beef, The Squirrel and The Buckmaster found an auto race on the TV. The rest of us were playing a game of euchre at the

THE FISH OF A THOUSAND CASTS

table. The motor home was starting to get cluttered with beer cans and assorted snack packages. I decided to light a cigarette.

"What are you doing?" asked The Squirrel. "I can't have it smelling like smoke in here, my old man will kill me."

"It already smells like stale beer," I said, "what's a little smoke going to hurt... I'll blow it out the window."

"Lighten up Squirrel," Beef jumped in, "we'll get this cleaned up before we get home."

Beef stood up to get a glass out of the cabinet and inadvertently knocked a can of beer over. The stale liquid ran onto the counter top, some of it dripped on the floor.

"Now you've done it!" squealed The Squirrel.

"It was an accident... I couldn't help it!"

The Squirrel gnashed his teeth and hastily tried to mop up the smelly ale.

"Here, I'll give you a hand with that," Smiley offered. He started towards the bathroom to get another towel and just as he was reaching for the doorknob with his left hand, Dickens burst from the door. The doorknob whacked Smiley square in the knuckles.

"Which one of you sicko's forgot to flush!" shouted Dickens. "It reeks in there!"

Smiley was jumping up and down waving his hand. The Squirrel started fretting over the bathroom door.

"Is it broken?" he asked.

"Naw," answered Smiley, "I think my knuckles are just bruised."

"I was talking about the door knob, you idiot!"

Smiley was certainly taking his lumps during this trip. His eyebrows were gone, his face was beet red and now his fingers were so swollen that they looked like toes. It was his wedding ring wearing hand of course.

"How is married life going to kill me if you guys beat it to the punch?" Smiley questioned.

The rest of the evening unfolded the same way. The Squirrel fretted over every little thing, Beef continued to spill everything he could, and the rest of us smoked cigars and played cards. As we drifted off to sleep that night, The Buckmaster gave Smiley some words of encouragement.

"Hey Smiley," he said, "16 hours until the execution!"

Everyone *except* Smiley laughed himself to sleep.

The sun was starting to come up when I awoke Sunday morning. We decided to head down to the river for a bit before taking Smiley back to his impending death sentence.

"Dead man walking!" Wally shouted as we walked down the trail to the river.

The rains from the night before had brought the water level up a few inches. As the sun started to break in the east, we could see images breaking the surface of the river current. I casted an orange wobble glow into the river and felt the tap tap tap of my sinkers dragging the bottom. Suddenly, a fish hit with such authority that it almost ripped the rod from my hand. I set the hook and a brilliant summer Steelhead vaulted from the water.

"Fish on!" I hollered. Wally made a cast just upstream of me and soon was into a fish of his own! I landed my fish, released him and quickly made another cast. Everyone else was casting orange wobble glows and hooking fish. The raised water levels had brought in a fresh run of steelies and they were hungry! We were the only ones on the river and this action of a lifetime was non-stop. We quickly lost track of time. It didn't seem like very long before someone asked what time it was.

"It's 12:45pm," said Dickens.

"12:45?" yelled Smiley. "Holy Cow! I'm dead!"

We all realized that it would take us two and a half-hours to get back home.

You've never seen seven guys sprint up a trail as fast as we did. Without taking our waders off we jumped into the